I0835250

The Dark Vision

By

Marjo De Vroed

ISBN: 9781958842638

Library of Congress Control Number: 2025949165

First Published by *Hamley Books*, Belgium, 2022
Published by *Spooky Ink Books*, Southwick, MA, 2026

www.AMInkPublishing.com

Spooky Ink Books is a division of *AM Ink Publishing. Spooky Ink* and *AM Ink* and its logos are trademarked by *AM Ink Publishing.*

Prologue

Ten years ago:

Rowin walks down the long, narrow hallway towards the kitchen. The old wooden floor creaks a little under her bare feet, but she pays no attention to it. Her nightgown flutters around her small body, which is still warm from sleep, and her raven-black hair falls in strands along her face. She doesn't know why, but she has to go to the kitchen.

She hears the soft shuffling of slippers running back and forth across the bluish stone floor, and before she can even see it, she knows who is in the kitchen: Grandma. After what seems like an eternity but in reality is only a few steps, she reaches the doorway. She wants to enter the kitchen cheerfully, when out of nowhere the doors of all the kitchen cabinets open and close. Amazed, she looks at Grandma, who is standing by the stove and doesn't seem to notice anything. She wants to warn the old woman about the strange cabinets, but her throat is constricted and no sound comes out. The doors start rattling louder and wilder, creating gusts of wind that make the raven-black strands of hair dance around her head.

She doesn't understand why Grandma doesn't notice the impending doom she feels. Fighting her fear, she tries to enter the kitchen where the doors are now rattling so loudly that even if she could scream, no one would hear her at all. To her horror, she sees how her grandmother turns away from the stove, staggers, and loses her balance. Then she slowly sinks to the floor, straight into the emptiness of the open kitchen cabinets.

Her grandmother and her mother come running to the screams of the little toddler, who is totally upset in her bed. Her forehead is soaked with sweat, and she looks around frantically as her mother lifts her from the bed. She is only three years old, and she has no idea how to explain to her family what she has seen. She just wants one thing: to be with the person she was unable to reach in her dream. Longingly, she stretches out her little arms to her grandmother. Like a little monkey, Rowin folds her body tightly around her grandmother as she takes her over from her mother with soothing and comforting sounds.

All the while Rowin repeats only three words, "Don't go, Grandma."

Sobbing, she lays her clammy head in the neck of her grandmother, who has turned pale around her nose. Rowin does not understand her mother's startled facial expression, nor does she understand the meaningful look the women exchange.

"Do we have a seer under our roof then, Moree?" she hears her mother ask softly.

"I hope not, Gwinnor, but I fear we do," her grandmother answers in a whisper. The two most important women in Rowin's little life do their best to comfort her, but it takes a long time before she calms down and dares to close her eyes again.

A week later, her grandmother is dead.

***

Present:

A strange, vague shadow hovers along the winding dirt road. The trees around him seem to bend slightly to the side by some inexplicable force. The moon shines on their tops, which are hardly bare anymore. Every now and then the phantom stops for a moment as if hesitating. He stays neatly on the path, unaware that he could float anywhere without encountering any resistance. He is neither fish nor fowl. Not a ghost and not a living subject. He hangs out in between everything: he is nothing.

He knows nothing either, only his name. The agitation, which hangs over him like an invisible shadow, tells him that he must find something. He just doesn't know what. He is a restless soul who does not know what he is looking for.

If he were to encounter a human now, they would think there was a strange patch of fog hanging over the path. Only the animals know better. Rabbits raise alarm by thumping the ground with their hind legs and then hurry off. An occasional fox darts away among the undergrowth along the path. Even the smallest mouse does not show itself in the silent forest, warned by a justifiable fear handed down from generation to generation.

The phantom does not seem to notice. He floats on towards a destination he does not know, towards a goal he cannot clearly remember. Only when he has passed the last trees does the forest dare to breathe again. The cruel Count has passed through.

Chapter 1

Rowin languidly looks out the window. The sun shines warmly on her left shoulder and the blue sky invites her outside. A blackbird hops back and forth, looking for insects hiding under the mostly bare, forked branches. It won't be long before spring erupts in all its ferocity and more young leaves appear on the trees.

"Rowin Kelsie!" Gwinnor's voice sounds stern. "Please answer the question."

More disturbed than startled, Rowin looks again at the old-fashioned blackboard hanging on the wall of the education room. Usually, she follows her mother's lessons without grumbling, but today the outdoors beckons. The tricky sum written in white chalk on the board fails to get her attention.

"Can we please do biology today?" begs Rowin. She points to the twittering sparrows perched in the hedge of the little graveyard behind their house. "Then I would pay much better attention than I do in this class."

"It's not even summer yet," Gwinnor sputters. "Am I supposed to stop teaching math classes altogether when the sun is shining?"

Rowin wisely keeps her mouth shut. When your mother is also your teacher, it's sometimes best to keep quiet. Anyone who is homeschooled knows that.

Rowin watches Gwinnor unconsciously grasp the amber stone that, shaped like a drop, hangs from a chain around her neck. Puzzled, her mother begins to roll it back and forth between her fingers, something she always does when she is thinking. Rowin is sure that, now that spring is about to come, her mother suffers from the same restless feeling as she does. For not only do their names recall their Irish past, but their love of nature betrays that they are descendants of the ancient druids from the land of their distant ancestors.

Rowin guesses that winter has knocked a big hole in her mother's supply of potions and that she desperately needs new herbs. The sun has been shining a lot this past week so, if she's lucky, Gwinnor will be able to find calamus, spearmint, and wild garlic. In a week and a half is the spring equinox: that day in spring when day and night are exactly the same length. It is an important holiday for druids. Before then, her mother probably wants to get her entire supply in order, so Rowin guesses that it will suit Gwinnor if she goes out now.

As soon as her mother lets go of the chain, Rowin knows she has made up her mind.

"How about I make you a concentration potion?" asks Gwinnor, looking at her daughter innocently. She can't resist teasing Rowin a little more before letting her go outside.

Rowin shakes her head vehemently no. Her mother's drinks are always effective but never tasty.

"All right then, you can go outside. But on one

condition: I haven't prepared a biology lesson," Gwinnor admits, "so I want you to go to Rufus. Ask him to explain the flowering of bulbs and annuals." She tries to look stern.

Rowin doesn't even notice. She has already slammed her books shut and is sliding her chair back. She wants to get out as quickly as possible, before her mother changes her mind.

The long, high corridor, with the old paintings of deceased relatives on either side, does seem longer than usual. Or maybe she's just more impatient. She takes the worn steps of the spiral staircase down two steps at a time. The fresh scent of spring tingles her nose as soon as she opens the door to the garden. She pulls the zipper of her coat a little higher, the gentle spring breeze feeling colder than expected. Zombie, her little dog, is already waiting for her and happily jumps up against her. The agreement with her mother is that he stays outside when she has class. Not because he pees in the house, but because he distracts Rowin too much during class. Rowin herself thinks it's because her mother can't see him. For her grandmother can read minds by touching someone, and her mother can make potions for anything and everything, but only she has the gift of seeing dead people and animals.

A gift that revealed itself when she was six and that has caused her to finally have friends in their big, lonely house on the outskirts of town. Though white and translucent, they were still true friends. "Because if you can see the future and talk to dead people, living friends are no longer an option," her mother always says.

Zombie gently taps his nose against Rowin's hand. He wants to play. The tingle of his touch brings back memories of her sixth birthday—the night she first saw the ghost of her grandmother, sitting on the edge of her bed. That strange, spectral-white appearance of her grandmother had brought Zombie for her as a present.

When this funny, semi-transparent dog enthusiastically gave her a lick and it seemed like a hundred butterflies with barbs on their legs fluttered against her skin, she knew he would become her very best friend.

She smiles at the fond memory of that birthday from long ago. Tomorrow she will already be celebrating her thirteenth birthday.

"Want to play, boy?" she cheerfully asks the wildly tail-wagging Zombie. She picks up a stick and throws it as far away as she can. With barking that only she can hear, he runs after it, and although he will never be able to pick it up and bring it back to his owner, it doesn't diminish his enthusiasm.

Rowin happily chases Zombie down the hill that their house is built on. She crosses the large lawn at an angle and walks toward the small graveyard that flanks their garden. There, bordered by an evergreen hedge, lie the graves of her relatives who used to live in their house.

The rickety, wrought-iron gate that hangs between the two low, dead-straight conifer hedges protests when Rowin opens it. She whistles at Zombie to call him to her, as if he couldn't slip through the closed gate on his own. The gravel, which runs in winding paths along the graves, crunches under her shoes. She should really rake it again, she sees. That would be job number 395 on her long list of tasks she doesn't feel like doing.

Only when Zombie runs in front of her between the graves does she close the gate. Following the path, she walks across a patch of grass to a small headstone with the inscription: "Here lies our beloved daughter Cara Comrádaí Kelsie, 1953–1965." She taps modestly on the stone and waits as Cara's ghostly head appears above the grassy area. As soon as she sees Rowin standing there, a grin appears on her pale, translucent face.

"Is it that late already?" Cara floats up from her resting place until she is fully visible.

"No, I got time off from my mother. But I do have to go to Rufus to ask him about some things."

Cara puffs up her cheeks. "Pooh, glad it's you and not me."

Rufus is the friendly gardener, who is so long-winded that you almost fall asleep of boredom when he is talking to you. He is the only non-family member buried in their graveyard. He worked all his life on the house's estate and lived in a simple, small house next to the barn on the property. He always said himself that he had never married because he loved the estate too much, so when he died everyone agreed that he was somewhat of a relative and should be interred at their graveyard.

Rowin rolls her eyes dramatically. "I had to say yes. The alternative was staying inside, and I didn't feel like it with this beautiful spring weather." She takes a step toward the gravel path, loudly sniffing the scent of early spring.

"Okay, we're apparently going to walk our noses now?" giggles Cara as she follows her friend up the gravel path. "You do know mine isn't working so well anymore, right?"

Rowin chuckles at Cara's joke, but her eyes are serious. She looks at the even features of the pale face next to her: a beautiful, classic face that looks like it was sculpted from white marble. Rowin once claimed that Cara looks almost like a Roman statue that walked out of a museum, to which Cara reacted with a ten-minute giggle fit.

"What a crazy idea, that tomorrow I'll be older than you'll ever be?" Rowin blurts out.

"Okay, nice of you to remind me of that," Cara says delicately.

With a slight blush, Rowin turns her head away. They're good friends, but this was an awkward subject to bring up. Sometimes she doesn't think before she says something.

"I'm sorry."

"Doesn't matter." Cara looks at her friend. "But how will that work when you get older and older?" The small thought wrinkle above her nose shows her concern. Long ago, in a secret ritual they made up themselves, they had promised to always be friends.

They had even exchanged a drop of blood, but now Rowin had unintentionally brought up a subject that neither of them had thought about until now. Cara will always be twelve years old, while Rowin will grow older every year. That thought seems to change everything.

"That makes no difference to me. We'll always be friends!" states Rowin decidedly. She raises her index finger in the air and puts her hand on her heart. Cara does the same and gently touches Rowin's finger, causing a gentle stinging tingle.

"Friends forever," they swear simultaneously as they solemnly look at each other.

Chapter 2

On the small hill in the middle of the graveyard stands a huge beech tree, stretching out its branches as if to protect the residents and their graves with mighty arms. Right there, the girls see Rufus standing with his behind up and his nose on the ground. They swiftly duck behind the largest headstone.

"He probably spotted a rare flower or something like that," Cara giggles.

"Or an interesting piece of moss," Rowin grins. "Anyway, I don't feel like being lectured about his latest discovery or flower bulbs or whatever." She puts a finger to her lips, and they silently sneak away before the ghostly gardener notices their presence.

Only when they are at a safe distance does Rowin dare to call out to Zombie, who has stopped by one of her great-aunts for a petting and a hug. The graveyard is full of great-aunts and old aunts-who-are-not-aunts, but what else should you call them? They stroll along the path past the hedge and Rowin looks sideways at her house. From here it looks old and dilapidated with its crooked, green shutters. The neglected stone walls separating the front steps from the garden have collapsed. The wild vines growing along the facade gives the house a ghostly appearance in autumn, but now it shows a green haze of budding leaves. How different it looks at the front, where the large driveway gives the house a stately look and where the rose bushes that bloom beautifully in summer brighten the exterior. Only someone who approaches close enough can see the large cracks in the wall that reveal the age of the building.

The house has been in the family for centuries through inheritance from mother to daughter. Only the last resident, who was called a witch by the villagers, had no children. Therefore, it went to her niece Gwinnor, Rowin's mother. Rowin has lived there with her mother and grandmother ever since she was born. Technically, from the age of three she has only lived here with her mother, because her grandmother has lived in the graveyard since then, but that's a small detail. Rowin loves her home just like she loves her graveyard and all the family that lies there. Can a person say that they love something as morbid as a graveyard? Without noticing, she shrugs. She can say whatever she wants. After all, there's not a living soul around who could think she's crazy.

"Why do you shrug?" Cara asks curiously.

"I was thinking about all of our family here and how much I love our graveyard."

Cara nods in agreement. "So do I. But sometimes I do miss eating ice cream or walking around the neighborhood." She ponders into the distance.

Rowin nods understandingly. She would miss that very much as well if she were dead.

Lost in thought, they walk on. On the way, they

cheerfully greet their relatives as Zombie happily plays tag with a couple of young children.

"Do you miss your father, Cara?" The question comes out before Rowin even notices.

Cara slowly shakes her head. "No, I didn't really know him. He left when I was a year old. Why?"

"Well, we were talking about missing out and then I thought… It doesn't matter. Never mind." Rowin makes an uncomfortable gesture. It's a subject never talked about at home. She doesn't know her father and her mother always says she didn't miss out on anything. Still, she'd like to meet him to see if she might have inherited her nose from him, or those four black dots under her eyes, which her mother says are freckles but which are also under her other eye in exactly the same spot. She knows that her bright blue eyes are a characteristic of her maternal family, because you can find those same blue eyes in all the portraits hanging in the hallway of their house. But her long, raven-black hair that makes her so distinctive belongs to no one but her.

"Say, Rowin," Cara breaks the silence. "What would you rather…"

The words linger in the air as Cara suddenly holds still. The expression on her face doesn't bode well. Rowin hesitantly turns her head towards the spot her friend keeps staring at.

On the grass between two headstones stands a small and crooked figure. She carries a basket filled with herbs on her arm. Her face is as white as Cara's, but that is where the comparison ends.

Between the deep-set beady eyes, a crooked hawk's nose keeps watch above a mouth turned to a narrow line. Her fluffy hair, which looks as if it houses a nest of young bats, hangs down in long strands. Rowin's heart skips a beat. This is the woman the villagers used to scold for being a witch. She doesn't meet her often in the graveyard, and that's fine with her, because secretly she's afraid of this ghost. It always feels like this woman is angry with her because she now lives in her house. Of course, that doesn't make sense, because if the old woman hadn't wanted them to live there, she shouldn't have made her mother an heir either. And yet there is always something threatening about her.

"Aintín," Rowin says. Her voice shakes slightly as she bows her head. Her mother has always urged her to greet their great-aunt with respect when she meets her. Aintín says nothing in return. Her pinhead eyes pierce right through the girls, which is not so difficult with Cara.

When Rowin looks up again, Aintín has raised her free arm and is pointing her finger towards the sky. Automatically the girls look up, but there is nothing special to see there. The finger begins to spin in circles, and on the ground some abandoned garden waste spins along with it, as if a small whirlwind were blowing quietly over the ground of the graveyard. Aintín's face remains expressionless as now her whole arm spins along and the leaves on the ground make a rustling sound. Rowin feels a shiver run down her spine as the woman stops her arm with a brusque movement. The garden waste turns motionless. Menacingly, her finger continues to point at the sky. The girls don't dare look at each other in fear of screaming. Rowin intuitively seeks Cara's hand, which yields only a faint tingle.

"Yeah, I'm taking off," Cara whispers, "too scary for me." Rowin looks sideways, startled to see her friend dissolve into a translucent cloud, leaving her alone. Meanwhile, Aintín's finger points at her and writes something in the air. A one and a three. Thirteen. The unlucky number. The number you won't find in any hotel. The number for the superstitious.

The age Rowin turns tomorrow.

Chapter 3

"Nice friend you are," Rowin grumbles to the small tombstone.

Cara is nowhere to be seen. After Aintín drew the figures in the air, Rowin had run away in fear. She's not a hero and she never will be, that's for sure. Her mother always grumbles that something as simple as Bambi stubbing his toe sets off her waterworks, and when scary music sounds in a children's movie, she avoids looking by immediately diving behind a pillow.

"Cara?!" Rowin gives a vicious slap on the headstone.

"I'll wait until you're not mad at me anymore," a hollow voice sounds from the grass. "Tomorrow on your birthday I'm sure you'll forgive me for this more easily."

"Maybe I will, maybe I won't." Rowin stares at the grass in exasperation. She knows Cara is right. She hates arguing and always tries to keep the peace with both her living and dead relatives. She picks up a pebble lying next to Cara's stone and throws it back onto the path. The stone protests with a loud *clack* as it lands among its fellow pebbles.

Rowin lowers herself onto the grass and sits with her back against her friend's small headstone. The encounter with Aintín still makes her knees feel very weak, and she can't seem to get the image of the pointed index finger pointing at her out of her head. Thirteen. What exactly did Aintín mean? It could hardly be a coincidence that the mysterious woman was indicating her age tomorrow exactly today, though she absolutely cannot imagine why.

A soft tingle at the crown of her head causes her to look up, straight into the familiar face of her grandmother stroking her head. Her grandma's literally eternal friend Madam Curiosa is standing behind her, curiously looking over her shoulder.

"What a deeply worried mind," Grandma Moree says softly. She rests her hand on the side of Rowin's head and looks intently at a point in the distance. "I see you've run into Aintín. Is that what's bothering you?" Madam Curiosa takes a few steps forward so as not to miss anything about her answer. "Well, well. I see you brought the walking tabloid," Rowin grumbles inwardly, but not softly enough.

"Tiens, chérie," sounds the high-pitched voice of Madam Curiosa. Her eyebrows are raised high, and she looks genuinely surprised, "What-te else you expect in such a teeny tiny little graveyard? If zère is-a any sensation-e here, we are-a happy!" Rowin has to chuckle at the honest words of the French-speaking lady. Her accent makes everything just a little bit funnier, yet there is no one who laughs at her for that. That also contributes to the nice atmosphere in this place. Nobody makes fun of you or looks at you in a funny way if you are different or can do something special, unlike the village children in the past. A couple of young boys had thrown stones at her from the road next to the graveyard when she was playing hide-and-seek with Cara. They had yelled and screamed that she was a crazy witch and then had run away. Fortunately, the stones had been small, but they were still big enough to make one lose faith in living children.

"It's nothing, Grandma," Rowin reassures her. "I'm seeing ghosts again." Giggling at her own joke, she plucks some small twigs from her pants. Madam Curiosa lets out a high and bell-like sound. "Aahh, you little z-jokester," she calls out, coquettishly slapping her fan in front of her face. "You must be zé funniest one at-a home, non?" Her dress rustles as she puts her arm forward and waves her hand back and forth in front of Rowin's face. Rowin smiles kindly at her. She has a soft spot for the lady in the beautiful dress, even if she is a bit meddlesome at times.

"By the looks of it, you're doing a little better. Then I guess I'll see you again early tomorrow morning? You know, on the one day of the year when I show off for you." Moree gives her granddaughter a wink before turning to her friend. "What do you think, shall we go for another walk?" Kindly, Moree extends her arm to her friend.

"Mais naturellement!" Madam Curiosa hooks her arm in Moree's and stiffly armed, they walk on, excessively gossiping about anything and everything.

Smiling, Rowin watches them until she feels goosebumps rising on her arms. The sun was nice and warm when she sat behind the window, but now that she has been sitting on the ground for a while, she is cold through and through. She stands up stiffly. Her legs are no longer wobbly, just a little rigid.

With a stroke of the small tombstone, she says goodbye to her best friend. She longs for home, for a warm mug of tea from her mother, filled with herbs that calm your mind and don't taste dirty.

Though that last one might be a bit much to ask.

Chapter 4

As soon as Rowin opens her eyes the next morning, she senses that something is wrong. Like every morning, she hears her mother rummaging in the kitchen downstairs. So she hasn't woken up from the birthday song that her grandmother usually sings first thing in the morning next to her bed.

That's strange, because she has never skipped a birthday since she was six years old. There is an ominous silence in her room.

Rowin looks beside her. Zombie is just lying quietly in his dog bed. On a whim, she throws her legs out of bed and walks across the cold floor to the window. A watery sun shines on the large beech tree of the graveyard. Moree's grave is to the right of the tree, but her grandmother herself is nowhere to be seen. Restless, Rowin turns and looks at the large grandfather clock next to her bed. Luckily it can't strike anymore (otherwise she wouldn't sleep at night), but it still shows the time.

Half past eight! Her grandmother has never been this late. She quickly walks over to the chair where she threw her clothes the night before and hurriedly gets dressed.

Zombie watches as she hops on one leg trying to put on her shoe without falling. Only when she throws open her bedroom door and runs out into the hallway does he lazily emerge from his dog bed and stretches. Not waiting for Zombie, Rowin storms down the stairs and, in passing, snatches her jacket from the coatrack. Only at the entrance to the graveyard does she get her zipper closed, yet she feels no cold. It is dead quiet at the graveyard when the gate creaks open. She feels a fit of panic coming on, preventing her from thinking logically.

"Grandma?" she calls out shrilly.

No answer.

She runs in one direction out of the blue, driven by a pressing feeling. Every headstone she encounters stands abandoned. No one chatting or gossiping about the neighbors. No one cleaning or caring for their stone. Everything is empty and silent.

It is not until she has reached the hill that she sees the white cloud made up of the graveyard residents. They flock together in the far corner of the graveyard like moths drawn to a flame. Her slight panic fades away now that she has found everyone, her initial fear now turning into curiosity. A lot calmer, she walks the final steps to the crowd.

She hears Madam Curiosa's high-pitched voice above the buzz of the other voices. That means her grandmother will be standing close by.

"Grandma?" she calls out again. The back of the flock turns around nervously and makes room for the human child who can see them. Their faces seem less pale than usual, as if an excited blush has befallen them.

Rowin looks around in amazement. She has never seen her friends like this before. They look like a bunch of excited children waiting for the bus to take them on a school trip.

Rowin walks quietly through the crowd towards where she heard the high-pitched voice. In the middle of the front row she spots her grandmother, with Madam Curiosa less than half a meter away. Only when she stands next to them does she see the cause of the excitement: where two conifer hedges mark the boundary of the graveyard and meet in a corner, there is a strange kind of fog. Not an ordinary fog, the kind you often see hanging over the meadows in the morning that makes the cows seem to float because it obscures their legs. Nor is it a cloudy, bright white fog that you can get lost in.

They are dingy, oppressive patches of fog, which muffle everything and give you goosebumps on your arms. And barely visible in those long patches of fog, a shadow flickers.

Chapter 5

"Grandma, what's going on?" Rowin doesn't even notice that she's whispering.

Moree makes a hand gesture that suggests she will not or cannot answer.

"Who are you?" From the impatient tone, Rowin hears that this is not the first time her grandmother has asked the phantom this question. "If you don't answer, we can't help you."

The excited murmurs of her dead friends buzz in Rowin's ears. She doesn't quite understand what this means. She knows that a spirit is bound to the place where its bones lie. Usually, that's in a cemetery or occasionally in a place where someone has died and not yet been found. But a ghost can't just visit another cemetery, as this ghost is doing now. In fact, Cara and the other spirits of her graveyard can't even make it to their house if no close relatives live there anymore. So how can this spirit roam freely?

She carefully looks at the patch of fog. Now that she looks at it more closely, it doesn't look like a ghost either. The outline of a man does flicker in the patches, but she doesn't see a real person like her grandmother or the rest of the graveyard dwellers.

"I ask you to leave if you have no intention of saying anything," Moree says decidedly. "As long as you do not make your intentions known, you are not welcome."

For a moment, the shadow flickers more clearly. Rowin sees a man in clothes she knows only from history books and paintings. He was apparently wealthy during his lifetime, for his coat is trimmed at the sleeves with ornaments, as are the lapels of his coat and the stiffly upright collar. The pants he is wearing are tight and even his boots are decorated with embroidery.

The mouth of the phantom opens and closes for a moment. Everyone is silent, waiting tensely for what the phantom is going to say, when the patches of fog make him fade away again.

"Graaaateemaaaa… I seeeek…"

It is a soft lilt, no more than a light summer breeze that carries the sound of rustling leaves from afar, but it gives Rowin the creeps. Moree has her head tilted and slightly forward, as she always does when she is listening intently to something.

"What are you looking for?"

"Don't know… must be… beyond…"

"Is Gratema your name?" Moree sounds impatient.

"Couuunt…"

The graveyard is empty. The dark gray sky stands out sharply against the few headstones still standing. Most of the stones are broken and scattered here and there. A haze that stiffens you to the bone floats over the plowed ground.

Startled by the ominous sound of scratching nails over stone, Rowin turns her head in the direction of the noise. A giant, black wolf is scratching its paws across Cara's fallen headstone. Her heart skips a beat when, in the corner of her eye, she sees black shadows coming out of the forest, spreading over what's left of the graveyard. More huge black wolves try to topple the few stones left standing by pushing against them with their entire weight. A few dig a pit to get to Cara's bones. The wind howls around her ears, or is it a wolf after all? Horrified, she sees how one of them has managed to dig up a bone from her friend. Her empty stomach turns over and she tastes the sour taste of stomach acid in her mouth.

She must have made a sound, because with a jolt all the heads turn in her direction. The biggest wolf raises his lip and shows a set of gleaming teeth. Yet that's not what scares her. It's the eyes. His blood-red eyes, staring at her hollowly and coldly.

She must have let out a big scream, because her friends are staring at her, worried. Rowin has fallen to the ground, her entire body shaking. The phantom is nowhere to be seen anymore; she must have scared it away with her fearful scream.

"Child, what is it? You look as pale as Cara!" Grandma bends down and looks inquisitively at Rowin's face. She gently places a hand on her cheek but pulls it back in horror as she takes in the image Rowin has seen.

"I… It… The graveyard. It was empty and everything was broken," Rowin stammered to the other spirits, who don't have Moree's gift and are waiting impatiently for what she is going to say.

"There were big shadow wolves with red eyes walking around who ate everything… And they ate your bones!" Filled with horror, her eyes shoot for a moment to Cara, who has been thrust forward in panic by her friend's primal scream and is now sitting next to her, trying to convince herself that she is all right. At the thought that Cara will no longer be there, Rowin almost panics. She has always been told that when the grave and bones of a spirit are destroyed, that spirit has reached its true end and disappears forever.

"It was like I was dreaming, but I wasn't asleep. I was really there! It was a vision." Rowin suddenly jolts forward, as if just now fully realizing what she has seen.

The ghostly crowd murmurs restlessly and some of the graveyard dwellers gesture aghast with their hands.

"A vision-e?" Madam Curiosa's eyes grow large. "Zhat is not cood. Moree, zhat is not cood! She sees into zhe future, nah?"

Moree shakes her head in disbelief and squeezes her eyes shut. She cannot comprehend what her grandchild has just seen.

"Are you one hundred percent sure of what you saw, Rowin?" Cara's voice shakes a little.

"One thousand percent."

"Is our graveyard in danger of being ransacked by big, red-eyed wolves?"

A suppressed cry sounds from the crowd, followed by the restless shuffling of worried spirits.

Rowin nods. She wants to go inside to her mother. To crawl under the covers and hide. She doesn't want to see these images again, only she can't turn them off like she normally would with a scary movie. They just keep haunting her mind.

"Is this really going to happen, Grandma?" Rowin looks at the deep frown running across Moree's forehead. "Am I getting daytime visions now instead of prophetic dreams, as Madam Curiosa says?"

"I have no idea, my dear, but if you are having visions, then things are not looking good for our graveyard. Indeed, then you have seen the demise of our resting place."

Rowin wants to get up, but her first attempt to regain control of her knees fails miserably. Even her teeth begin to take on a life of their own, chattering as if it were ten degrees below zero. Did she really just see a flash of the future? Or did she perhaps make it up? She has never seen wolves like that before. In fact, she didn't even know such beasts existed.

"I think it would be better if you went home, Rowin," Moree says emphatically. "You look as if you might faint at any moment. Cara, you walk with her just to be sure."

Cara stands up and waits patiently for Rowin's body to listen to her again, so that she can remain standing without faltering. She holds out her hand as if Rowin can take it. The gesture alone is so reassuring that she follows Cara willingly.

As soon as the startled Rowin is out of sight, an overwrought crowd pours a waterfall of questions over Moree.

"What does her vision mean?"

"Who's been targeting our graveyard?"

"Is it the fault of that Gratema?"

Moree raises her hands. “I don’t know. I wish I had an answer to all your questions, but I’ve never experienced this before and neither has Rowin. I suggest we let her recover a bit, then I’ll go to her in a moment to find out what this is all about.”

Under slight protest, a number of the residents wander off in disappointment and seek their own spots again. Others cling to each other and form groups that spread out over the graveyard to discuss the doomsday message at length. Only Aintín remains, watching from a distance. Her eyes look into Moree’s. Slowly she raises her arm, clearly writing the number thirteen in the air.

Chapter 6

"Where did you go?" Gwinnor looks in surprise at her shivering daughter, who stands absently and pale in the doorway of the dining room. The table is festively set with croissants, cookies, cake, and deliciously sweet toppings. Rowin's chair is decorated with garlands and on her plate is a package with a bow wrapped around it.

"To the graveyard."

"Why?"

"Grandma wasn't here this morning to congratulate me, so I thought something was wrong." Rowin feels her bottom lip quiver. "And I was right."

Her mother rushes over and puts an arm around her. "My poor girl, what happened?" She calmly leads her to the table and gently sits her down on the decorated chair.

With a lump in her throat, Rowin tells her mother what happened at the graveyard and how she can't get the images of her vision out of her head.

"Oh, poor child," her mother soothes. "How shocked you must be. And on your birthday! Shall I make you a cup of soothing tea?" Rowin nods. She doesn't care what nasty drink her mother is brewing right now, as long as it helps her get the grim images out of her head. She is startled when, in the corner of her eye, she sees a white shadow in the doorway. To her relief, it is her grandmother.

"Are you all right?" asks Moree cautiously. Rowin nods meekly. Her grandmother steps into the dining room and looks at her with concern.

"You do understand that we have to do something about this?" Moree sits down at the one spot of the table where there are no decorations. Not because she gets tired standing, but because she knows it makes her granddaughter feel at ease. In recent years, their best conversations always took place as they sat casually around the table.

Rowin squeezes her eyes shut. "No!" She says it so loudly that her mother spills some tea.

"What the…" Gwinnor wipes up the spilled tea with a cloth. "Is Grandma here?"

"Yes, and she says we have to do something with my vision," Rowin says in a panic.

"I'm really not going to do anything with all this scary stuff, Mum! You know what a scaredy-cat I am, right? I don't dare!"

Moree looks straight at her granddaughter. "You've seen for yourself what those terrible wolves will do. You can no longer claim not to know what will happen, Rowin. To me, there is no question that it has something to do with the Count. As soon as he hung around our graveyard, you got your vision. We may not know exactly why, but one thing is certain: if we do nothing, our graveyard will be lost. Is that what you want?" Moree shifts uncomfortably back and forth. She knows it's not fair of her to pressure Rowin like this, but she also doesn't know anyone else who can help her save their graveyard. Only Rowin, as a living person, can see ghosts and talk to them.

Depressed, Rowin looks at her grandmother and takes a sip of the tea Gwinnor has given her. Slowly she shakes her head. "No, I don't want to," she says stubbornly.

"What does Grandma say?" Gwinnor lets go of the chain around her neck, which she has been unconsciously twisting. She puts both hands around Rowin's face and softly wipes her thumbs along the four dots under her daughter's eyes to catch the rolling tears.

"Don't cry, dear. You should use the gift you have been given. Your name means Predictor in our ancient language for a reason."

Rowin sniffs and wipes the last of the wetness from her eyes with her sleeve. "What should I do?" she asks her grandmother softly. Clearly relieved, Moree stands up. "We as residents can't get out of the graveyard to look for him, and your mother can't see ghosts. So you are our only hope of finding the Count." Her grandmother looks at her kindly. "Sorry dear, but you will have to go after him and find out more about him."

"How?" With wide eyes, Rowin looks at her. "He only mentioned his name, not where he's from. How can I find out where he is now?"

A tingle in her hand makes her look down at her legs, where Zombie is enthusiastically jumping up against her. Absentmindedly, Rowin strokes her little friend. He spins around under her hands, each time bumping his nose against the palm of her hand.

"Stand still for a moment. I can't pet you if you…" Rowin stops in the middle of her sentence and looks at Moree, a wild plan roaming through her head. "Zombie!" she shouts. "Zombie might be able to follow the Count's trail!" The little dog wags his tail even harder than usual because of his owner's enthusiasm. He has no idea that he has just been promoted to tracker dog.

***

Gwinnor walks with Rowin and Moree to the graveyard, where everything seems quiet again.

Rufus is carefully examining the moss on his own stone and Cara is walking happily towards them with one of her little nieces on her arm. If you didn't know better, you would think nothing had happened.

"Are you all right again?" Cara looks at Rowin inquiringly. She nods affirmatively. Cara nods back in relief. "I'm glad," she says contentedly.

Arriving at the hill, they see only Madam Curiosa still standing on the spot where the shadow had appeared that morning.

"Aaah, tiens. Zhere you are!" she says cheerfully.

Rowin has no idea whether she's talking to her or to her grandmother, so she smiles back kindly.

Zombie hops happily in front of her, barking

excitedly at the only ghost he sees there.

"Zombie," Rowin calls him to order, "come over here." She walks to the far corner and drops to her knees. "Listen, boy. You have to do something you've never done before, but I'm sure you can do it. Find the phantom for me."

Zombie stares from one to the other with his tongue hanging out of his mouth.

"Are you sure he can do it?" asks Gwinnor doubtfully.

"If you don't believe in him, then go away," Moree sneers, momentarily oblivious to the fact that Gwinnor can't hear her.

Rowin points to where the phantom has been standing and taps the ground a few times. Curious, Zombie comes over to take a look. When he doesn't seem to do anything but wag his tail, Rowin picks up some soil and brings it to his nose. "Search!" she says decidedly.

For a moment, Zombie hesitates. He sniffs at her hand, spins around and sticks his nose in the air. Then he wags his tail enthusiastically and darts under the hedge.

"He's got a trail!" cries Rowin, surprised and excited at the same time.

Moree takes a startled step backwards as her granddaughter jumps over that same hedge with a great leap. As soon as Rowin stands with both feet on the dirt path, the excited feeling flows away and doubt strikes. She has never walked beyond the graveyard.

The idea of going who-knows-where on her own doesn't entice her at all. In the distance, Zombie is already running ahead down the dirt road.

"Do you guys really think I should go after him?" asks Rowin hesitantly.

"Yes, of course you should go after him," Moree presses her on. "Go quickly, before you lose sight of him." Rowin nervously runs a hand through her sleek, black hair and heaves a deep sigh. "Off you go, then."

"Maybe you'll come across an ice cream parlor," Cara tries to encourage her. "If you do, will you bring me an ice cream?"

The joke works, as a tentative smile breaks through on Rowin's face. "I'll also bring a spoon for you, which you can't hold," she jokes back shakily. Then she straightens her shoulders, takes three deep breaths and runs.

"Be careful," Gwinnor calls after her, but Rowin doesn't hear her mother, already too far away down the path to her new adventure.

Chapter 7

The stinging in her side makes Rowin pant. For the first part, she ran across fields and small winding roads chasing after Zombie, but soon her fitness let her down. Maybe she should ask her mother to teach gymnastics too.

They have been walking in the woods for more than half an hour now, and it doesn't look like Zombie is going to stop anytime soon. She can't take any more. Rowin looks at her phone to see what time it is. Almost half past eleven. They've been on the road for two hours.

Her stomach rumbles softly. It wasn't smart of her to run after Zombie without thinking twice. She should have thought more carefully about it. Then she could have packed lunch and taken her bicycle with her.

The wind rustles through the heavy branches of the pines, the only trees that are green here. Where the deciduous trees are, the forest is bare and transparent, but in this part the conifers, with tall ferns at their feet, create a dark and impenetrable patch of forest along the path. Rowin feels the shivers run down her spine. She looks down the path, searching for the small, white dog who so enthusiastically follows the scent trail of the Count. He is nowhere to be seen.

"Zombie?" Her voice sounds shrill and is muffled

by the density of the large trees. Uncomfortably, she looks around. Next to her, a pinecone plops to the ground and her heart skips a beat. "Zombie?"

She turns around in a flash when a branch snaps behind her. "Who's there?"

Rowin blinks her eyes a few times to better spot any potential attackers. She looks for a large branch to defend herself with, but the pines have left nothing for her. It seems like shadows are moving in the darkness of the forest. Her heart beats uncontrollably in her chest as she tries to calm herself. "Your head is playing tricks with you," she mutters. She repeats the words until she almost believes them herself, meanwhile moving along the path like a ninja with her back arched and her arms out in front of her at a ninety-degree angle. With each step she looks around, wary of unexpected danger.

Only when she hears Zombie barking does she drop her caution and straighten up again.

"Where were you?" Rowin tries to blink away the tears of relief burning behind her eyes. Zombie jumps up against her and happily wags away her anxious thoughts. "You're a little monster," she says playfully but angrily, "Now remember, don't run so far ahead!"

As soon as they leave the forest, Rowin sees a church tower in the distance.

"Are we headed towards a village?" She is surprised that a ghost would want to live among people.

She knows from her grandmother that a ghost despises when a human walks through it, and in a village you can't always avoid people. She runs after Zombie at a trot, afraid of losing him again.

Before they even get close to the village, Zombie turns into a narrow side road. He wriggles under barbed wire and runs up a hill toward a tall hedge before suddenly stopping and barking.

"Where did you take me?" Rowin mutters. She follows him, walking curiously along the hedge. Peeking through it, she vaguely sees some plants and flowers on a marble slab. "A cemetery!" Excitedly, she pushes the hedge a little farther apart. There are headstones behind the hedge that look very different from her graveyard. As far as she can see there are marble memorials, large tombs, and even small houses in this place.

"Wow, you see those little houses, Zombie? Those are mausoleums. Sometimes a whole family lies in them. And I don't mean poor slobs like you and me. There's only people with money lying here by the looks of it." Rowin whistles admiringly through her teeth. "I think I was right and our phantom was a rich man. Come on, let's find the entrance."

Zombie turns his head towards her. For once, his owner gets to lead the way.

There seems to be no end to the hedge that surrounds the cemetery. When she can finally turn a corner, Rowin sees the stately entrance looming a little farther ahead.

Two tall, stone columns hold in place a gigantic wrought-iron fence, which has a gracefully rounded top and is decorated with lavish scrolls. In each pillar is a square, black stone, where the solemn Latin texts *Memento Mori* and *Tempus Fugit* are engraved in gold letters.

Rowin tilts her head slightly and thoughtfully squeezes her eyes shut. *Remember to Die* and *Time Flies*, she quickly translates in her head. She always grumbled during her Latin classes because she was sure she was never going to need that ancient, dead language. Now she is grateful that her mother forced the boring material onto her.

The large gate is closed, but next to it is a smaller entrance with an open gate. Two people come walking out and Rowin takes a step aside to let them through. As soon as they have passed, she slowly walks inside, impressed by the many imposing tombs that stretch almost side by side before her. Each one is more beautiful than the last. Even the most magnificent tomb in her graveyard cannot match the simplest one here. There is no gravel, but all the paths are paved and meander neatly from left to right up the hill, so you can get to each grave with dry feet.

There are no people in the cemetery and yet it is very busy with the dead. Many spectral women in beautiful, full dresses with lots of ruffles and ribbons are standing around talking to each other. A few are waving their fans, not to cool themselves but to disappear coquettishly behind them. Because the ladies don't know that Rowin can see them, they automatically step back while chatting to let her through.

Rowin is absolutely blown away. Fortunately,

Zombie barks softly at her, as she almost forgets why she is here. She rushes after him as he runs up the hill between the structures. Meticulously, she dodges every graveyard dweller she encounters, much to the surprise of many. Once at the top, Rowin remains stunned. As busy as it is down the hill, it is quiet up here. There is only one square building on the grass, and it is so large that it doesn't leave space for many other graves on the hilltop. The imposing mausoleum resembles a white, Roman temple, with triangles as roofs and Doric columns all around. In the center is a short, wide staircase that leads to a tall, black door.

"No way," Rowin whispers. "He hasn't lied. He really is a Count. Who else could afford such a gigantic mausoleum?"

She brushes away a black tuft of hair that sticks to her sweaty forehead. Then she sighs deeply and walks slowly to the mausoleum. Uncertainly, she puts her foot on the first step of the marble staircase. She wants to run back home, but remembering her vision, she knows she has no choice.

Zombie is waiting impatiently at the top of the stairs for her. He has walked straight to this building.

There is no doubt: the phantom is behind this large, black door.

Chapter 8

Carefully, Rowin pushes the door open. The musty smell of wet wood and rotting potatoes greets her as her eyes adjust to the darkness. The only light comes from the narrow windows high in the roof. In the center of the mausoleum, she can vaguely see two tall, marble rectangles on which lies a human form. She doesn't really want to go inside. She feels her heart pounding in her throat, making it seem like it's being squeezed tightly. Nevertheless, she takes a step forward and walks over the threshold onto the uneven floor tiles.

Inhale through your nose and out through your mouth. That's what Gwinnor used to tell her when she'd had another scary dream and crawled into bed next to her mother in a panic.

Rowin closes her eyes for a moment and follows the wise words. Just like before, she feels herself becoming calmer. After a long exhale, she resolutely steps towards the tombs.

She has never seen this kind of tomb before. Hesitantly, she walks past the tomb and looks at the beautiful clothing and the details in the white stone faces of the man and woman who lie there so quietly and beautifully immortalized next to each other. Rowin bends over the statues a little. They look so real, she could swear she sees the Countess moving. When the marble woman slowly blinks her eyes, Rowin lets out a scream. A ghostly white figure rises from the stone, floats to the corner of the tomb, and sits there silently with her hands in front of her eyes. Despite the fact that her legs feel like cooked spaghetti, Rowin takes in the spirit with interest. She sees how the Countess' back curves and how her shoulders jerk violently. She is crying, she realizes. Her fear gives way to compassion and curiosity.

"Are you all right?" she asks kindly.

The spirit lowers her hands a little, allowing Rowin a glimpse of her wet eyes, but she immediately hides her face again behind slim, white fingers. The jerking of her shoulders continues. No tears fall down, not even spectral ones. Rowin doesn't know how to posture herself. She wants to comfort the woman, but she doesn't know how. Hesitantly, she takes a step forward.

"Ma'am?" Rowin leans forward to look at the Countess. To keep her balance, she presses her hand against the tomb, causing an unexpected flash.

The thick walls behind the Countess are sand-colored and wallpapered with a beautiful tapestry. It shows a romantic scene by a forest lake with young men, smiling women, and beautifully shaped horses in the foreground. The Countess stands in front of it as she shouts, "No, not my child!" Her hair hangs in tufts around her head, loosened in a heated struggle. She holds the arm of a boy who is wildly resisting. Her knuckles are white from clenching, and her fingers bore deep into the child's flesh in a desperate attempt to hold him to her. The kid tries to kick a man who wants to pull him away from his mother. To the Countess' left, another man appears and grabs her violently. One by one, the man loosens her fingers. Her high-pitched scream cuts right through the bone as she feels her last finger loosen and she loses her grip on the boy.

Overwhelmed, Rowin takes her hand off of the tomb. The Countess has removed her hands from in front of her face and holds her mouth open as if in a silent scream. Horrified, Rowin looks at her. What has happened to the boy? In the mausoleum there are only two tombs: the Countess' and the Count's.

Where is their son's tomb? Did she overlook it?

"Countess?" she asks cautiously. "What has happened to your son?"

The Countess sadly turns her head away and floats back into her tomb without saying anything.

"Well, she clearly doesn't want to talk about it," Rowin concludes. She peers intently down the four walls of the locked room. Other than a few decorative vases and some porcelain figurines that probably belonged to the Countess, she sees nothing. No tomb, no grave, no urn or memorial plaque. Not even a small elevation in the floor where a boy could possibly be buried. There is nothing at all that looks like a grave for the child.

She doesn't get it. Why is the Countess a ghost, her child gone, and the Count wandering around like a phantom? She had been sure she would find the Count here. Zombie had led her here with his sharp nose for a reason. Okay, the tomb is there and so is his wife, but where is the Count?

"Think, Rowin. Think!" Impatiently, Rowin slaps her forehead with her hand. She tries to remember the Count's words. What had he said again? He had given his name: Count Gratema. And he had said something about the Beyond. She understands that much. He is obviously not a spirit yet, for then he would be clearly visible. So he still has to cross over to the Beyond to become a spirit. When a person dies, his soul crosses over to the Beyond, unless he has unfinished business here.

Could that be the Count's problem?

Rowin closes her eyes to concentrate even more. She can almost reach the memory that hangs in her head like a thin morning mist. Come on! What else had the Count said?

Then it suddenly comes to mind.

"I seek!" she shouts. "That's what he said." Zombie is startled by her unexpected cry of triumph and runs out of the mausoleum with his little tail between his legs.

Rowin looks excitedly at the Countess' tomb. "That's it! The Count has something to finish on this Earth before he can become a ghost. He's looking for someone and thanks to you, I know who." She straightens her coat and decisively thrusts her chin forward at the Countess. "I will see to it that your son is returned home and that your husband can go to the Beyond. I'm sure that's the way to get everything right again. Then you can lie reunited in the mausoleum with your family, your husband will be happy and won't send wolves to our graveyard, and then no graves will be looted and that wretched vision of mine will have a happy ending."

Chapter 9

Starving, Rowin attacks the croissants, which have dried out somewhat from waiting on the kitchen table. She spreads a thick layer of jam to compensate for the dry texture, having just enough self-control not to munch loudly.

"So, it really is a Count," Grandma concludes. "A wandering soul in search of his son, according to you."

Rowin nods with her mouth full as she tears the wrapping off her birthday present, which she hadn't had time for that morning. She'd almost forgotten it was her birthday today.

"Oh, Mom, thank you." She holds up a book by her favorite author admiringly. "I really wanted this one."

Gwinnor smilingly accepts an enormous embrace. "And now?" she asks, impressed by the story about the cemetery. "How are you going to find that son?"

Rowin shrugs. "No idea, actually. I promised the Countess I'd find her son. I just don't have a clue where to start." She takes a big sip of the herbal tea in front of her. "I was hoping you could help me."

Her mother looks thoughtful. "You should never make a promise if you're not sure you can keep it. And this is a very heavy promise."

Rowin shrugs her shoulders. "It was out before I

knew it. You should have seen the Countess, Mom. She was inconsolable," she says, trying to justify her promise. "I'm sure you would have done the same."

Gwinnor raises an eyebrow but says nothing.

"I used to go to Lordensland often," Moree muses. "Listening to your story, I think you've been to Noblesse Rest, the cemetery of Lordensland. It's large, full of ornamental graves and is just outside the village. If the Count is buried there, he must have lived near it, right?" Moree looks at her granddaughter questioningly.

Rowin quickly puts the mug of tea, which she was just about to bring to her mouth for another sip, back on the table. "Well done, Grandma! That really helps me," she says, praising her grandmother's train of thought.

"What?!" asks Gwinnor, impatiently sweeping a few crumbs from the table. Usually, Gwinnor has no problem with not being able to hear conversations between her daughter and her mother, but Rowin can tell she's finding it very annoying at the moment.

"Granny thinks our earl lived in Lordensland, or at least in the area." Rowin hurriedly gets up from the table and quickly stuffs another piece of blueberry muffin into her mouth. "So guess what I'm going to google now."

Rowin is almost nose deep in her laptop, having put her nearly dead phone on the charger. With rising amazement, she reads about the village, which this morning she didn't even know existed.

Lordensland is a historically important village, which was at the center of a conflict over land borders between two landlords: Count Gratema and Count Landis. The former ruled with an iron hand over Lordensland and its surroundings. He claimed all the forests and the game living there for his hunting parties, including the part that belonged to the estate of Count Landis. On several occasions there were fights. When the tenants of Gratema, driven by hunger, revolted against his inhuman regime, Landis seized his chance and supplied weapons and soldiers. Gratema was driven out of his castle by the rebellion and lynched by his tenants. The castle burned to the ground.

Rowin shuts her laptop. She doesn't comprehend everything in the article, but she knows enough to understand that Count Gratema treated his workers so badly that they killed him. An uneasy feeling creeps up on her. Perhaps her mother was right and she should not have promised the Countess anything. The Count had not been a sweetheart when he was alive, so what if he didn't even want her help in the afterlife?

Rowin shakes her head decidedly. No, that wasn't an option. She'll have to ease the Count so that he'll leave her graveyard alone.

She grabs a piece of chocolate and puts it in her cheek, melting it nice and slow so she can enjoy it for a long time. It helps her think. Good. So, the Count had indeed lived in the area of Lordensland. Unfortunately, the article did not say exactly where, only that his castle had been burned to the ground, so she won't find much more on that.

On impulse, she opens the laptop again and types in a new search command: *Lordensland Castle Gratema.* Besides the website she has just visited, she gets even more hits. One of them, a newspaper article from the *Lordenslander Daily*, catches her attention. She clicks it open.

Find of the Century

By *Lordenslander Daily* Staff

During construction of the new shopping center Buyzz, the contractor has stumbled upon the remains of a ruin, likely the remains of a forgotten castle. The work will be postponed until further notice, and for the next few weeks archeologists will take over the premises for investigations.

Rowin looks again. Could it really be? The ruins of a lost castle! She looks at the date of the newspaper. February thirteenth. That's a month ago. Today is the thirteenth of March, the day of her thirteenth birthday. Without wanting to, she is reminded of Aintín. Her hand writing the number in the air. Thirteen. If she weren't so scared, she would go to Aintín and ask her if it was a coincidence.

"Have you found anything yet?" her mother calls from the bottom of the stairs.

"Your mother was impatient as a child too." Moree says quietly, leaning against the doorframe.

"Grandma! You really scared me," Rowin sputters. "But I think I've found something. At Lordensland, a ruin was found by construction workers. That could well be our Count's castle."

Triumphantly, she looks at her grandmother. A smile spreads across Moree's face.

"Well then, what are you waiting for?"

Chapter 10

Of course, Rowin's mother hadn't allowed her to go exploring yesterday. She had thought it much too late to go out (it had only been half past four!). She had wanted to make the rest of Rowin's birthday a pleasant one, which was understandable but not useful when you are so enthusiastic about your discovery.

Rowin almost got into a fight over it with her mother, but she remained patient and now she's on her bicycle in the pouring rain on her way to Lordensland. Unfortunately, Rowin couldn't make the journey in the nice warmth of her mother's car because she suddenly had to go somewhere else. The rain falls steadily on her head and despite her raincoat, she feels a drop slide down her back over her neck. Zombie doesn't seem to be bothered by anything and hops happily next to her.

The bike path leads her along the edge of the forest and not through it, like the dirt road she followed yesterday. And because there aren't as many pines on the outer edge, it's a lot less dark and scary despite the gray rain clouds. Maybe she had just been imagining things yesterday. She had the feeling that something or someone had been watching her in the woods and then that branch had cracked…

Rowin unconsciously starts to cycle faster. After all, you never know.

After some searching and asking around, she finally sees the big announcement sign for the new shopping center being built. It will be exactly on the other side of the village, in the opposite direction from the mausoleum. It looks ultra-modern in the picture, but Rowin doesn't like it. There are fences around the building site, and when she puts her bicycle up against them, two men wearing helmets walk past her, heading for the shack a little farther on.

"I swear, it's haunted over there," one of the men says nervously. He has a small goatee that bounces up and down when he talks. Rowin giggles by the sight of it.

"Ghosts don't exist. How many times have I told you that?" the other man replies calmly. He pulls a handkerchief from his pocket and starts blowing his huge nose. "The men are just joking with you," he continues from behind his handkerchief.

Goatee stands still, offended. He waits until Big Nose also stops and turns to look at him.

"When those men of yours aren't even around," Goatee continues, "I still notice that things have moved. So how do you explain that?" His voice sounds like a fierce barking little dog, used to barking at everything and everyone.

Big Nose is not impressed. "You must have been distracted and moved those things yourself unconsciously," he says, shrugging his shoulders. He puts his handkerchief back in his pocket and walks on. Goatee follows him, trying to convince his colleague of his rightness with a shrill voice and broad hand gestures. Their voices quiet down as Big Nose opens the door of the shack and they step inside to get shelter from the rain. Rowin walks inquisitively along the fences lined with black plastic to keep intruders at bay. When she sees a large crack in the plastic at one of the fences, she peeks curiously inside.

A white mist hangs in the large pit that the construction workers have dug. It is thin enough to see the remnants of walls that the archaeologists have already uncovered. Rowin feels the fog fill the air around her, making it harder for her to breathe. Anxiously, she grips the fence. What is happening? She wasn't bothered by anything until she saw the fog. Zombie jumps up against her worriedly. *He would have made a good service dog*, she suddenly thinks. She strokes his head reassuringly.

"I'm all right, Zombie. I think I was just scared." Bravely, she walks on, though she doesn't feel that way at all. "There must be an entrance here somewhere. If we're lucky, all the archaeologists are in the shack taking shelter from the rain," she says more to reassure herself than her dog.

The entrance turns out to be nothing more than two fences that have been pushed apart a bit. One of the fences is broken, leaving a thick piece of iron wire sticking out in the open. Rowin carefully wriggles her way through it. Once inside, she feels the pressure on her chest increase again, but it quickly fades when she realizes what she sees. With her mouth open, she stares at gigantic white walls towering high above her. To her left and right, two towers look down on her. In front of her looms a large gateway, its doors closed. Two large, white metal rings hang down idly. This is no ordinary fog; this is the spirit of the castle!

Rowin remains standing, confused. How can this be? She has never been able to see a building that no longer exists. A building can't have a ghost, right? She notices that she has started breathing even faster, causing her to feel dizzy. Once again, the fence provides a handhold.

"Zombie," she whispers, impressed. "Do you see this too?" The little dog leans forward and barks excitedly.

"So yes," she observes. "Then at least I haven't gone mad."

As soon as Zombie stops barking, a faint cry for help is heard. Zombie barks again, but Rowin silences him. "Shhh, I hear something!" She turns her head slightly so that one ear is turned towards the castle. It remains silent. For a moment she thinks she has imagined it, but then she hears it again.

Someone is calling for help! Startled, she looks around but doesn't see anyone. It's still raining softly and she is sure everyone is in the shack.

"Hello?" she calls out in desperation. "Is anyone there? Do you need help?" She takes a few steps forward until she can see into the pit where the archaeologists are normally working. The rainwater is running down in streams, making the ground muddy and slippery. Rowin has to be careful not to slip and fall down.

"You can hear me! You can hear me!" the voice calls weakly. "I knew it when I saw you walking there with your little dog."

Rowin remains nailed to the ground. If someone can see Zombie, it can only mean two things: either there is someone down there who, like her, can see the dead or there is a spirit in distress.

"Where are you?" she asks cautiously.

"Here, down here."

Vaguely, in the far corner, she sees something moving that looks like a waving white flag.

"You see me! You really see me!"

Is Rowin just imagining it, or does the voice suddenly sound a lot stronger and triumphant?

Out of nowhere, she feels goosebumps spreading across her arms and all over her body.

It's the cold and the rain, she tells herself. Nothing more. She's just cold. Right?

Chapter 11

Rowin carefully puts a foot on the stairs the archaeologists set up to get down to the excavation. Step by step, she descends. The steps are covered in mud, making them quite slippery. Zombie stays behind under loud protest. When she looks up, she sees his head poking over the edge. After ten or so steps, Rowin feels solid ground beneath her feet again. She turns around and looks between the crumbling stone walls for the spot where she had seen something moving… and where something is still moving.

"Hello?" she tries to hide the fact that her voice is shaky. She doesn't quite succeed.

Without warning, the white shadow is suddenly in front of her. Rowin takes a step backwards in fright and feels the ladder pierce her back. A few inches away from her, a boy's face is looking at her suspiciously. Rowin estimates he is a few years older than her. He squints his eyes a little to take her in better. His compressed lips make his mouth a narrow line. His wild hair is untamed and jumps in all directions. Through a large tear in his shirtsleeves, she sees his muscular arms. The rest of his clothes look dirty and frayed. This could never be the son of a rich Count.

"Who are you?" asks the boy. "How is it possible that you see me?"

"I... I don't know. I've been able to see ghosts since I was six," Rowin stammers, not normally giving that kind of information to anyone. Her mother taught her that, but for the sake of convenience, she assumes it only applies to living people. "You called for help, right?"

The boy ignores her question. He floats away from her a bit, when suddenly he is in front of her again.

"What's your name?" He sounds almost curious.

"Rowin. And would you please stop standing so close to me?" she asks as politely as she can while her heart pounds in her throat.

"I'm Erris. And yes, I do think I can do that." Erris floats back a bit, not taking his eyes off her. "What are you doing here, anyway?"

"I'm looking for someone. To be precise, I'm looking for Count Gratema's son." Rowin tries to suppress a shudder as she watches Erris' face change from curious to hateful and back to curious again. It happens so quickly that she wonders if she saw it right.

"Really?" Erris sounds delighted. "Is someone looking for me?"

"Are you the Count's son?" Rowin could bite her tongue off now. Erris must have heard the surprise in her voice and seen the disbelief in her eyes. Judging by his appearance, she would have sworn he was a farmhand. In her vision, the Count's son seemed younger and looked a lot less shabby. "How wonderful that I found you!" she says quickly.

"Did my father ask you to find me?" Erris looks at

her suspiciously.

"Well, something like that," Rowin says hesitantly, "but he is looking for you. Do you find that hard to believe?"

"It's been so long," Erris muses. "I'd actually given up hope." Erris' gaze turns glassy and he stares at a point above her head. As he continues, he relives a day several hundred years behind him. "I was in the basement when I heard a lot of gunfire. It looked like the castle was under attack. No idea by whom. All I remember is a lot of noise and the smoke. Lots of smoke."

Rowin has no intention of sharing the information she read on the computer yesterday. The Count is welcome to tell his son what really happened.

Once Erris has shaken off the memories, he takes her in closely. "How do you know my father?" he asks sharply. "And why is he searching now?"

Rowin shrugs her shoulders. "No idea. Maybe he's never come across a living person who could see him. Or maybe because a shopping mall is now being built on top of your castle." She takes a better look at him. "Is that important? Aren't you glad he's looking for you and that I found you?"

Erris' distrust immediately turns to glee. "Of course I am! I'm very happy! Is my mother with him too?"

"Um… yes, something like that."

"So, he needs me to get to my mother?" Erris gives her a confused look. Is she mistaken, or is there slyness in his question?

"Yes. Only when he has found you can he rest beside your mother."

"Then there is not a moment to lose! If you take my bones, you can bring them to my parents and everything will be all right," Erris says, gloating.

Filled with horror, Rowin looks at him. She hasn't thought about that! Erris is not here voluntarily. He died here and can't leave because his bones are here. That means…

"No way am I going to dig up your bones!"

Surprised, Erris looks at her. "That's what you came here for, isn't it? To reunite me with my parents?"

Rowin suppresses a shudder. She can't bear the thought of having to dig up a body in the mud in this weather. She shouldn't be thinking about digging up a corpse at all. Her stomach protests violently and she feels a wave of nausea come up, which she tries to get rid of with a lot of swallowing. She has her head bowed and looks down at her sneakers, which are now completely covered in mud.

She lets out a long sigh and looks up again, straight into Erris' eyes. She wishes it weren't so, but he's right. There is only one way to get him into the mausoleum, and that is to take his bones before the archaeologists find him. Because if they dig up his remains, they'll probably put him on display in some museum, and then she'll never be able to reunite him with his parents. And if they are not reunited, then her vision will come true and the wolves will pillage her family's graveyard. With a deep exhale, she lets her shoulders droop.

"Where do you lie?" asks Rowin resignedly.

"Just follow me." Erris floats to the spot where he had called for help earlier. Rowin walks behind him doubtfully. She doesn't know why, but it doesn't feel right. Her heart flutters restlessly in her chest and she nervously looks up at the edge of the construction pit. Vaguely, a few questions settle in the back of her mind. Why had he called for help in the first place? And why was he in the basement and not with his parents upstairs when the castle was attacked?

There's no time to think it through: Erris has stopped. "Here. This is where I lie. Not very deep. I think you have to dig about one spade deep."

"One spade deep? Rowin has no idea what he's talking about. Impatiently, he points to a shovel in the corner.

"Yes, a spade, a narrow shovel. And hurry up a bit, because as soon as it's dry, those men will be back."

Rowin knows he's right. Reluctantly, she picks up the spade someone left behind and puts it in the ground where Erris points to. With each scoop she takes, she encourages herself.

Scoop.

She has no choice.

Scoop.

She has said "A" and now she must say "B."

Scoop.

She promised the Countess.

Scoop.

She has to save her graveyard.
Boink.

Chapter 12

Rowin shudders when she sees the creamy white color of a bone shining through the mud. Gagging, she turns around.

"Come on now," Erris says cheerfully. "It's not that bad. I don't even stink, because my flesh has already rotted away." That comment causes another gag reflex. With teary eyes, she puts the spade deeper into the ground so that it gets underneath the bone. This is how she once watched Rufus dig up the roots of a dead rose bush. Now, by leaning on the handle, the spade should tip the bone upward. It works, and following that strategy, Rowin digs up the bones one by one. She has placed a piece of tarp, one that had been stretched over other tools to keep them dry, on the ground beside her, and she carefully places each bone on it. In the center of the tarp, a small pothole has formed where rainwater collects, helping her to rinse the bones clean. When the skull appears, Rowin can no longer restrain herself. She turns around, removes herself from the scene by taking a few steps and throws up the entire contents of her stomach behind one of the dilapidated walls. With the sleeve of her raincoat, she wipes her mouth, while Erris looks at her amusedly.

"You're not used to much, are you?" Erris points to his skull and gestures for her to pick it up. "Have you never had to slaughter an animal to eat?"

"I'm quite comfortable with buying my stuff at the store, thanks," Rowin snaps back. She picks up the spade, scoops the skull into it and lets it roll onto the tarp. "And digging up corpses isn't really my favorite activity. Do we have all your bones now?"

Erris nods. Rowin grabs all four corners of the tarp and ties them together like a knapsack with a piece of string she found among the items under the cloth. As she tries to hoist the bag onto her back, she lets out a groan.

"How much did you weigh?!" she roars.

"Do you always complain that much?" grins Erris. "Come on, I'll help you."

"Yeah, sure," Rowin grumbles as she walks to the stairs with her heavy load. At the top, Zombie is growling as if his life depended on it. "They're only bones, Zombie," she tries to calm him as she puts her foot on the first step. As soon as she starts climbing, she feels the weight pulling her back, but after three steps the knapsack gets lighter and lighter.

"I'm definitely getting used to your weight," Rowin groans contentedly. She is unaware of the evil grimace of Erris, who stays behind her and pushes against the bottom of the bag with two hands.

"Easy!" Rowin puts the bag of bones on the ground and tries to calm Zombie, who continues to bark fiercely at Erris. "It's all right. This is the Count's son." Erris looks suspiciously at the small dog who is now growling at him as if he might attack at any moment. Rowin knows that Zombie can't attack people, but she doesn't know what it's like with ghosts among each other. She's not taking any chances.

"Zombie! Shame on you!" Punishingly, she waves her finger at his raised head and reluctantly Zombie drops off. "Sorry, he normally doesn't behave like this."

"It must be because you now have a bag of bones with you that he's not allowed to eat." Erris tries to make a lighthearted joke about it, but the sharp undertone in his voice doesn't really make it work. Rowin is too busy with the bag to notice.

"Good. At least we got to the top. I hope it will be as easy on the bike," she mutters. She swings the bag over her shoulder again and walks over the soggy ground to the fence. The rain taps her head a lot softer than it did earlier. She looks up at the lightening sky. She has to hurry. She must be gone before the men return to the dig.

Rowin wriggles through the fence again and comes to a halt halfway through with a jolt. The overstuffed tarp doesn't fit through the narrow opening and is still hanging on the other side of the fence. When she tries to pull the bag towards her, she cuts her upper arm on the sharp protrusion of the fence.

"Ouch!" She grabs the sleeve of her coat with a pained face, where the iron wire has made a large tear. Bright red blood creeps up through the hole, and a sharp pain pulls through to her shoulder.

"No time to fuss over a scratch," Erris says impatiently. "Hurry up now."

With tears in her eyes, Rowin grabs the tarp bag again and gives it a hard tug. The bones make a strange noise as they bang against the fence, but no matter how hard she pulls, the bag stays on the other side. It has almost stopped raining now, and in panic she looks toward the shack, where laughter can be heard. She has to hurry.

"What are you doing?" hisses Erris. "You'll break my bones if you go on like this."

"I'd rather have a few of your bones broken now than have those guys discover me and break all my bones when they see me running off with their precious council property later," Rowin gasps. Continuing to pull at the bag is useless, she realizes. She'll have to come up with something else.

"Then pull that fence farther apart," snarls Erris.

Of course! How stupid that she didn't think of that herself. She lets go of the tarp and pushes with all her might against the fence, which doesn't shift a millimeter in the heavy mud. The voices in the construction shed grow louder as the door of the shed opens slightly. A hand is put out fleetingly to feel how hard it is still raining before the door closes again. Rowin looks anxiously to the side, realizing that she has little time left. She pushes with all her might against the gate, which gives way a little.

"Higher," Erris orders.

In confusion, Rowin looks at him. "What do you mean?"

"At the bottom it's stuck in the mud. You have to

push the fences apart at a higher point. Then it will work."

Rowin tries to push at a higher point and the fences do indeed give way. The only drawback is that now she has no hand left to pull the tarp through. As if Erris can read her mind, he says, "You just make sure the opening is big enough, and I'll get the bag to the other side."

There is not much time to think. She hears the rumbling in the shed as the men get ready to go back to work. She puts her feet as high as she can against one side of the fence and leans with her back against the other side. She pushes the sides of the fence apart with as much force as her feet can handle until the hole is big enough to let the bag through. To her amazement, she sees Erris stand behind the bag and push it through the opening, but she doesn't have time to dwell on it for long.

The door handle of the construction shack moves again and slowly the door swings open.

Chapter 13

With an enormous jump, Rowin dives behind a large bush, helped by Erris, who gives the bag one more push. Rowin lies on her stomach on the ground. The bush is dense at the bottom, so she can't see where the men are. She doesn't want to know either. She closes her eyes and hears only her blood rushing and pounding in her ears as if she has run a marathon a hundred times. Her head is almost bursting with adrenaline.

"Get up!" orders Erris as he climbs down the fence. "Now is the time to run away."

It doesn't feel like Rowin's legs are going to hold her. She will probably fall to the earth after three steps with her weak legs and then the men will see her floundering helplessly and get angry at the thief and…

"Get up!" Erris is screaming now.

Rowin knows she's not going to get a second chance. She hoists herself off the ground and runs as fast as she can with the bag on her back to her bicycle. With trembling fingers, she ties the bag under her bicycle's carrier straps. It bulges over her carrier on two sides and she hopes it will stay put. Then she runs through the worst of the mud, holding her bicycle by the handles before jumping onto the seat and frantically pedaling away.

It has stopped raining and a hesitant, pale sun is breaking through the clouds. Rowin is far enough away from the construction site to pedal more calmly. The first stretch has whizzed by as if the Devil were at her heels. She looks around for the first time since the escape instead of staring sternly ahead. The heavy branches of the trees are still dripping from the rain. The forest floor is wet and soggy, and the intoxicating smell of mushrooms and soil fills her nose. It calms her in a strange way.

A little farther on she sees a rider on a steaming horse. It looks like the animal is on fire with that much steam coming off its neck. Would the rider see her too? She suddenly thinks of what it must look like; a sweaty girl on a bicycle with a gigantic overhanging bag tied to the back, on which an invisible spirit is lounging lazily with a small invisible dog tagging along beside the bicycle.

Involuntarily, she bursts out in laughter.

Immediately, Erris' face is beside her. "What's so funny?" he asks suspiciously.

"Nothing special. I was just thinking how I must look to an outsider." Rowin smiles.

"Where's my father?"

"And your mother," Rowin corrects him. She doesn't quite understand why he's only asking about his father. In her memory flash, his mother had clearly been upset when he was taken from her. "They're in the cemetery a little way down the road. We will follow a narrow path in a moment, and then we have to cross a meadow and we'll be there. I have to search a little, because we'll arrive from the opposite side now."

Erris' face disappears again, allowing Rowin to concentrate on the surroundings. When Zombie suddenly slips into a narrow path ahead of the bicycle with a sharp turn, she hits the brakes hard. The bag rattles and shifts forward a bit, but to her relief it stays put. She quickly follows her spectral buddy, who has already found the trail again. When she arrives at the meadow, she puts her bicycle against a white birch tree and removes the bag from under the carrier straps. Fortunately, she has tied it tightly and not a single bone has fallen out, she observes with satisfaction. In a moment the Count will be reunited with his son and he will be able to cross over to the other side. The Countess will be overjoyed to hold her son in her arms again and the whole family will live happily ever after in the mausoleum, thanks to her. And most importantly, once the Count has left for the Beyond, he will have no reason to send those black wolves with the blood-red eyes, so her family's graveyard will be spared from destruction. Job done, promise fulfilled, calamity averted.

Rowin swings the bag to the other side of the barbed wire and dives under it herself. Zombie is already at the hedge. The gate is familiar territory by now, as is the place behind it. The rain has apparently scared off many of the cemetery's residents, because it's not nearly as crowded as the last time she was here. Rowin chuckles. Apparently, there is such a thing as fair-weather ghosts, who like fair-weather people only come out when the sun is shining. The few who do show up look suspiciously at the girl smiling to herself with the orange bag on her back.

Pleased with herself, Rowin climbs up the hill to the lone building at the top. Erris is nowhere to be seen. She suspects he's just as excited as she is and maybe even nervous, since he's going to meet his parents again after such a long time.

Zombie is already barking on the stairs in front of the door when she arrives at the hilltop. With a smile, Rowin opens the door to the mausoleum. The Countess is sitting on the edge of her tomb again, and in the corner she can see patches of the Count's fog. With a triumphant gesture, she puts the bag on the ground in front of her and begins to fumble at the string that holds everything together. The rain has made it stiff, so it takes extra effort to loosen the knot. She feels the spot where she cut her arm open on the fence burn with the effort.

"Dear Count and Countess," she begins, gloating. "May I present to you: your son!"

Proudly, Rowin pulls the string from the tarp, causing the four corners to fall down and reveal Erris' bones.

It remains deathly quiet in the mausoleum. In the distance, Rowin hears a church bell strike. The Countess' face changes from sad to puzzled. In the corner, Rowin sees the fog flicker and the Count's figure clearly outlined against the dark wall. Exactly as she had hoped.

Then, with a *bang*, the door slams shut behind Rowin. Startled, she looks back. What is happening?

Who slammed the door?

"Héllo, Fáther." The sarcasm drips from Erris' voice. Slowly, he emerges from behind Rowin and holds still next to her. First he looks at his father and then at his mother, challenging them both.

In the corner, the Count is looking at his son with a clearly impassive face. The Countess has fallen to her knees and is looking up pleadingly at her son. Rowin looks from one to the other, startled.

"What… what is going on here?" she stammers. This is not at all what she had in mind when she walked in here. She had expected joy, for the prodigal son had been found again and everything would be all right now. Instead, the tension is palpable and no one is smiling.

"Erris!" It sounds ice-cold. The Count is now a lot more visible, and he has found his voice again. But his eyes do not radiate love, as Rowin had expected.

"I hear you have some unfinished business here on Earth," Erris scoffs. He hovers back and forth in front of Rowin with a disdainful smile. Each time he passes by, Rowin feels the tingle of his closeness and the hairs on the back of her neck stand up. She looks at the Countess, who is still on her knees, her arms wrapped around her chest while rocking gently back and forth, as if comforting a baby.

"No, no, no." Rowin shakes her head

incredulously and keeps her arms spread, as if to keep a bunch of hoodlums apart. "This is not how it should go." She speaks hastily and almost trips over her words. In confusion, she looks at the ghosts one by one. Then she points determinedly at the Count.

"You are looking for your son, and once you have found him, you can go to the Beyond. That is how it is. That is how it must be. I brought your son to you, so why are you still here?"

Chapter 14

"Oh, dearest father!" Erris tilts his head slightly and makes a pouting face. "Can't you go to the Beyond without your little son? Is he your unfinished business? Is he the reason you have to stay here?" The snide, sarcastic tone frightens Rowin.

The Count doesn't get hot or cold about it. He continues to look down on his son haughtily. After half a minute of tense silence, he flickers slightly and seems to become less visible.

"Oh no!" shouts Erris furiously as he surges forward. "You're not leaving! The first time I force you to think of me again since you left me to rot in that dungeon, and you make yourself scarce?!" Erris spits out the words and his face radiates hatred. "It feels wonderful that you can't leave now because of me."

Rowin takes an uncomfortable step backwards towards the door. Erris looks like a lunatic who will stop at nothing to get his way. What has she done? Her whole plan has failed. What's more, by the looks of it, the Count is in a lot more trouble because of her.

As his father fades even more, Erris loses his self-control. He throws his head back and raises his arms with his fingers spread wide. One of the vases standing along the side begins to vibrate and suddenly flies toward the phantom in the corner. With a *bang*, the vase explodes against the wall a few inches from the Count. In a reflex, Rowin impulsively holds her arms in front of her eyes as she feels the shards fly past her face. Slowly lowering her arms, she realizes in horror why Goatee thought the excavation was haunted and why the tarp bag felt so light on the stairs. Erris has telekinetic powers and therefore can move objects without touching them! She had seen it at the fence, but in the rush she had not paid attention to it. What a colossal mistake!

The Count, by her shielding gesture, notices the rip in her sleeve and the bloody wound beneath it.

Becoming slightly more visible again, he asks with a worried face, "Did Erris do that?"

Rowin doesn't understand what he means at first, but when she sees him pointing at her sleeve, she shakes her head in denial.

Erris makes a hollow, grim smile. "So, you have to be a stranger to get you worried, Father? Rest assured, I have not touched her. This child is nothing more than a means of transportation to me. A handy pack mule who could bring me to you. But I can honor my bad reputation and torture her a bit, if you prefer?"

In less than a second, Erris is standing next to Rowin, who suddenly feels a great pressure come to her chest, just as it did that afternoon at the dig. Her breathing becomes more difficult and she becomes dizzy. Zombie barks fiercely and tries to bite Erris' legs. Rowin hears a dull thud as the villain kicks the little dog against the wall with a well-aimed foot. Zombie remains still, crumpled on the floor.

"No!" The Countess' high-pitched cry cuts through marrow and bone. "No, let her go!" Desperately pleading, she raises her hands to her son from her position on the floor. "Not again. Not like before. I beg you, Erris."

As soon as Erris lets the pressure on her chest ease, Rowin falls to the floor on her hands and knees. She gasps whoopingly, causing her to cough violently and feel like she's choking. Her throat burns and tears roll down her cheeks as she drops to her side.

Erris looks at his father with a triumphant look. "Don't look so shocked. I let her live. That's more than you did to me. You let me languish in that dungeon for years and then let me rot there for another two hundred years."

Without taking his eyes off his father, Erris paces back and forth with clenched fists. The Count follows him intently, wary of another outburst from his son.

"Children who take pleasure in gouging out the eyes of animals or cutting off fingers from their staff are a danger to the world, Erris." The Count is clearly visible now and apparently remembers everything again. In a clear voice, he continues, "You left me no choice but to protect humanity from your diabolical nature. You owe everything to yourself. And that you have been imprisoned for two hundred years was not our fault. The enemy killed me unexpectedly and set fire to the castle. I did not abandon you. I never stopped looking for you, though I was not aware of it until recently."

"And that makes everything okay?" roars Erris. "So now you think you can cross over without a problem?" His words are cold as ice and his face is hard as stone. "Forget that, old man. I've dreamed every day for two hundred years that I could take revenge, and believe me, I'm going to! Your time to cross over will *never* come."

Before Rowin realizes what is happening, Erris raises his arms again. From the ground, a whirlpool of sand and stones emerges, which he slowly sends towards his father. The Countess' screams cause Rowin to take action. She has to get out of here! Erris has shown that he has dangerous powers that she can't compete with. She looks to the side and sees Zombie still lying motionless against the wall. She swallows heavily as she tries to push back her rising tears. She has no time for that now.

Hampered by the swirling sand and rubble, she tries to locate Erris. Her hands shake and her legs feel weak, but then her instincts take over as she focuses on the rubble and sees that Erris is too busy with his father to pay attention to her. She estimates the distance between her and Zombie to be three paces. She looks back at the door Erris has slammed shut. It will take some delay to open it, but if she is quick, she should be able to make it out before he realizes what is happening.

Rowin tenses her muscles and counts down in hushed tones. She looks up through her eyelashes at

Erris one more time, and when he's not paying attention, she jumps up from the ground, sprints to Zombie, snatches him up, and runs for the door. Terrified and in a hurry, she grabs just next to the door handle with her trembling hands. In the corner of her eye, she sees Eriss' head turn towards her. In a panic, she grabs for the latch again and fortunately this time she has more luck. Before Erris can stop her, the door flies open and Rowin, with Zombie under her arm, runs out of the mausoleum.

Rowin has no time to be careful. She runs like mad across the cemetery to the exit, running right through the single ghostly person that doesn't jump aside in time, leading to great displeasure and grumbling as she pushes through their phantasmal form. She does not hear it. She can think of only one thing: that she has to get out of here. In her arms, Zombie moans softly, the heavy shaking bringing him back to his senses. Rowin is glad to see that he's still alive, or at least something like that. After all, a ghost is already dead, right? But she knows very well that a ghost can also meet its end, and fortunately for Zombie that time hasn't come yet.

This time the gate with the beautiful fences is wide open, waiting for a funeral procession to bring a new resident. Relieved that she doesn't have to slow down for the narrow pedestrian entrance, she runs through, finding the hedge she must follow. She gets painful stitches in her side and her panting makes every breath cut into her dry throat. She ignores the pain as much as she can. Now she must go through the meadow to the barbed wire. She forces herself to squeeze out one last sprint. The grass hides the uneven clay underneath, causing her to stumble. She tries to keep her balance with a few big steps, but there is no escaping her stumble as she falls forward.

Clutching Zombie tightly, she rolls a few feet through the wet grass and slips under the barbed wire, which stings viciously in her shoulder and thigh. She falls halfway onto the road, but when she wants to get up quickly, she feels a tug on her head: the barbed wire pulling her back. A large strand of her raven-black hair is tangled in one of the iron pins. In a panic, she pulls as hard as she can on the tuft of hair, but it only seems to get more firmly stuck. Forcing herself to calm down, she pulls on the tuft of hair with one hand while holding on to the barbed wire with the other. Now it works. A few hairs remain, but she breaks free. For the first time, she dares to look back to see if Erris might be following her. Fortunately, she doesn't see him anywhere. He is probably too busy bothering his father. She lays Zombie down in the basket on the front of her bike, puts her feet on the pedals and rides away.

When Rowin is almost home, a terrifying howl can be heard from the forest as pale, translucent wolves prowl toward the cemetery.

Chapter 15

Rowin comes running down the driveway, shouting loudly. Startled, Gwinnor clambers down the stately staircase to the main entrance, taking two steps at a time. She arrives at the front door just in time to catch her pale child as she stumbles off her bike and plucks something invisible out of her bike basket.

Gwinnor grips her soaking wet, shivering daughter tightly and helps her up the stairs.

Moree, too, has heard the shouting and hurriedly comes running. Together they look shocked at the muddy, bleeding wounds on Rowin's body and at the dirty, tangled raven-black hair that sticks to her face.

"My goodness! What has happened to you?" Inwardly, Gwinnor curses the appointment she had that morning, which had prevented her from driving her daughter to Lordensland. Now she feels terribly guilty.

In the large hall with the huge mirror, Rowin is startled by her reflection. Her mother quickly pulls her into the kitchen so she has no time to dwell on her battered appearance. She guesses that the invisible package that Rowin carries so carefully is the little Zombie.

"Here, put him on here." Gwinnor pulls a towel from the drawer and places it on the kitchen table. "Is he all right?"

Rowin nods resignedly. She carefully lays Zombie's still-limp body on the table before Gwinnor takes off her coat and pushes her into a chair. Moree comes up behind her and strokes her head comfortingly. Zombie whimpers softly and tries to wag his tail. Something snaps in Rowin as she sees her faithful friend lying there, kicked so hard he must be seeing black and blue. She puts her hands in front of her face. "I've ruined everything!" she cries with long exhalations.

"Don't worry about Zombie," her grandmother soothes. "He'll be back to his old self in no time, trust me."

"No, that is not what I mean," Rowin sobs. "I've ruined everything for the Count!" She removes her hands, and with her sleeve she wipes away the snot and tears that have gathered around her nose.

First she looks at Moree and then at Gwinnor. "I found Erris, the Count's son, and brought him to his father, only he wants nothing to do with his father."

She gives a summary of what happened that day. Gwinnor, who in the meantime is tending Rowin's wounds from the fence and barbed wire, gets a little paler with each sentence. "By Dagda! May our ancestors stand by us," she mumbles nervously, clutching tightly the amber drop on her chain, which represents the god Dagda's baton. "Is Grandma here, girl?" Rowin nods again.

"What does that mean, Moree?" asks Gwinnor, who has no idea where her mother is in the kitchen, so she just looks at Rowin, who Moree would surely be near to provide comfort.

"That means we have a problem," growls Moree. "The right question is: what should we do now?"

Rowin always feels like an echo pit when she has to interpret between the two worlds, but now she doesn't grumble and translates everything Moree says directly to her mother.

"If the Count doesn't pass," Moree continues, "our graveyard will be destroyed. No one knows exactly by whom or why, because she hasn't been able to see that yet, has she, dear?" She strikes Rowin's hair affectionately. "But what I do know, is that black shadows with red eyes, from wolves or whatever, usually don't have good intentions."

Moree stops for a moment and stands in front of Rowin so they can look at each other. Her face is serious. "The three of us have quite a few special gifts, but I'm afraid this one is beyond our capabilities. If Erris can stop his father with his telekinetic power, I don't know what your seer gift can do to counter that. And if the Count won't go beyond…"

A grim silence envelopes the room.

"But if my gift isn't strong enough, why did I get that vision of our graveyard?" asks Rowin.

"That means I have to do something, doesn't it?"

"That's exactly what I don't understand either," Moree says to no one in particular. "I only know of one person who might be able to help us, because she has the gift of wisdom." She looks obliquely at Rowin. "I just don't think you'll like it."

Uncomfortably, Rowin looks back. She has no idea who her grandmother is referring to, but she feels a strange itch in her stomach.

"You'll have to go to Aintín, dear," Moree says kindly but firmly. "And let's face it: after Erris, that will be a piece of cake for you."

Rowin nods in resignation. Somehow she had expected this when Moree said she wasn't going to like it.

"Can't you come with me, Grandma?" She doesn't want to nag or beg, but it seems a lot more pleasant to her if she doesn't have to go see Aintín alone.

Moree shakes her head. "No, sorry, girl. You're the seer of the three of us. You had the vision, not us." She glances sideways at Gwinnor, who is rocking back and forth restlessly on her feet. "Your gift is what matters. Aintín will know what to do and she doesn't need any prying eyes to do it. That will only distract her."

Rowin tries to stall as long as possible with another glass of lemonade and something to eat, but now she really has to go. Step by step, she walks down the long corridor and over the stone stairs. It feels like all the painted family members are looking at her, shaking their heads as if no one believes in her difficult mission. Her mother and her grandmother walk with her to the garden doors.

"Good luck, honey." Gwinnor gives her daughter an encouraging squeeze on the shoulder. "I'll wait for you here."

"You can do this. Remember: all our hopes are

pinned on you." Moree nods at her briefly. If Rowin hadn't been nervous already, these words were enough to almost send her into panic mode.

"Thanks, Grandma. Thank you for not pressuring me." If her voice hadn't been so shaky, it would have sounded sarcastic. Rowin stands still for a moment, staring into the distance. The light outside is already starting to dim, which makes her mission even more difficult. Aintín is already terrifying during the day, so you can imagine what she'll be like when daylight fades.

She takes three deep breaths and blows the air out through her lips. She grabs the door handle, opens the door, and steps out over the threshold. She stops and looks up for a moment. Thankfully, it is dry. At the end of the lawn, she sees pale figures walking across the graveyard. She realizes then that there is no point in delaying further. She will have to go to the graveyard and overcome her fear of Aintín. It has to be done.

She looks back once more, right into the expectant faces of her mother and grandmother, before stepping decidedly onto the path. Behind her, she hears soft whining and one moment later a familiar white shadow appears at her feet.

"Zombie!" Rowin can't help but shout out with joy that her faithful four-legged friend is feeling well enough to come with her. She bends down and Zombie yips softly. "Are you not in pain anymore, boy?" she asks, happily letting him wash her nose with tingling licks. Zombie barks briefly, as if to say, "I won't let you do this alone."

"Nice," Rowin says bravely. "Then we'll go to Aintín together. We have to save our graveyard."

Chapter 16

The squeaking of the gate sounds more dreary than ever. The ghostly white figures she saw walking around the graveyard a moment ago are nowhere to be seen now. Rowin wonders if they seem to know what's going on. Against her better judgment, she hopes she will run into Cara, so she doesn't have to go to her great-aunt alone. When Cara is around, she is always more brave. But her friend doesn't show up. She and Zombie will have to face this alone.

Rowin walks down the gravel path to the right, away from the stately tree in the middle. The gravestones here are less familiar to her than the ones on the left side of the graveyard, where Cara lies. They are older, too, and stand out sharply against the fading light with their mossy tops. Despite hardly ever coming here, she knows exactly where Aintín's grave is. Her grandmother took her around the graveyard when she was little to introduce her to all the residents so that she would be familiar with each spirit and his or her final resting place. When she sees the large, gray soapstone tomb looming ahead, she knows what it says even without good light: *Here lies our aunt Aintín Kelsie. May she rest in peace.*

The businesslike and detached notice on the headstone was the work of her mother. She had been responsible for handling the funeral of an aunt she had never seen or heard of. There was no love lost between the two of them, no real family connection that could have led to a warmer inscription. Just like Aintín had never warmed up to Rowin when Moree went to proudly introduce her after discovering her new gift at age six.

Rowin remains standing hesitantly. Zombie presses his little nose against her ankle in a friendly but coercive way. She sighs. Then she gathers all her courage and knocks on the gray stone.

Nothing happens. Rowin looks around to see if the old woman might already be outside. When she sees no one, she knocks on the stone again. Nothing. She doesn't know whether to be relieved or disappointed.

"Aintín," she calls softly as she knocks on the stone for the third time. Rowin can already see the air above the stone moving, even before her great-aunt floats out stately. Her wild hair spikes around her head like the snakes of Medusa, making her appearance even more terrifying. She takes in Rowin from head to toe, hovering around her like a ghost in a bad horror movie. Rowin almost twists her neck trying to keep looking at her.

"What do you want from me?" The old woman's voice sounds scratchy and reveals that she hasn't spoken in a long time. Yet her words do not sound unfriendly.

"I need your help. *We* need your help," Rowin corrects herself, glad that she has gotten her voice and her heartbeat under control.

Aintín looks at her suspiciously. "Who is *we*?"

"Mama. Grandma. The graveyard. The Count. Me." For a moment, Rowin can't think of anything more to indicate how badly they need her help.

Aintín lets out a disdainful snort. "You turned thirteen on the thirteenth of this month, in the thirteenth year of the wolf and thirteen years after my death. I knew that combination would bring misery. Everything pointed to it. But this..." She looks at Rowin impatiently. "You're not smart enough, girl, if you haven't realized by now that it's not just about you."

With a jerk, Aintín turns her back to the shocked Rowin, who sees her making incantatory gestures in the air with one hand and holding her tombstone with the Celtic cross with the other. She is mouthing words in a language Rowin cannot understand but which sounds surprisingly familiar. Confused by Aintíns words, she looks at Zombie, who has taken a few steps backward and is looking at her great-aunt with his upper lip raised. Rowin swallows a few times to moisten her dry throat. What did the old woman mean about it not just being about her? About who else then?

When Rowin looks up again, the remaining light has left the graveyard. Dark clouds have gathered and hang over her head like a black blanket. The bushes around them rustle and move briskly back and forth.

Aintín seems to be in a trance, constantly mumbling the same unintelligible words to herself. Just when Rowin wants to ask who else is involved and what she should do, the old woman abruptly turns around. Her eyes are turned away and only when Rowin lets out a horrified cry do they turn back.

Tightly, she looks at the frightened girl. “Go,” she says hollowly. “Stop the black shadow that wants to rule the world. You alone have that power. Stop the Count’s son, for starters, by burying his bones under a sacred oak tree consecrated by a druid. That is the only place for an evil spirit to find peace.”

For a moment she staggers. Fortunately, the stone provides enough support to keep her on her feet. She looks at Rowin as if she has just awakened and is surprised that the girl is still standing there. Her voice sounds a lot friendlier as she continues, “Go. You’re stronger than him. He suspects it, but he’s not sure yet. Open up and use your strength. Believe in your strength. Believe in yourself.”

Before Rowin can ask anything more, the old woman disappears into her tomb. The wind picks up even more and pulls at her coat. It is chilly and the black evening sky seems darker over the graveyard.

She doesn’t know if the uncontrolled trembling of her body is caused by the cold or by something else. Zombie barks. They have to go back.

“I know,” she reassures him. “I’m just not sure I understand what Aintín said. My question was simple, but her answer only raises more questions. What do you think?”

Zombie runs ahead a bit, stops, and turns around.

He seems to be urging her to keep walking. His head shakes as he barks three times.

"Yes, yes. Quiet! I'm already coming," Rowin mutters. She takes one last look at her great-aunt's gray tombstone. She hopes to see her for a moment, so she can ask the questions that keep spinning in her head, but the grave remains silent. Nothing moves. Or does it?

Rowin pays closer attention at the bushes a little way off. The wind pulls at the branches that swing wildly back and forth. Except at one point. The shadow is blacker there and nothing moves. As soon as Rowin realizes that something or someone is standing there behind the bush, the shadow disappears into thin air. Zombie won't stop barking and runs back and forth, panicking. Suddenly, she understands that he has been trying to warn her all along.

Rowin turns around in an instant and runs like a girl possessed up the path, following Zombie to the graveyard's exit. Is she imagining it, or does the shadow keeps following her? She doesn't dare to look. She can feel the shadow carefully making sure it stays in the dark, avoiding the bushes and tombstones. The hairs on her arms and on her neck stand up. She has no idea how it's possible, but she cannot only feel the shadow, she can somehow see it without looking sideways. It's like she's hovering above herself, peering down like a bird of prey. It frightens her.

At the end of the path, the shadow stands still. Rowin throws the gate open so hard it almost flies out of its hinge. She doesn't care. She has to get inside!

Chapter 17

"Not one hair on my head would even consider letting you go!" roars Gwinnor. She paces around the kitchen, occasionally pulling open a cabinet aimlessly just to have something to do. She has just heard her daughter tell a story that made her skin crawl, and since pounding on the old stone stairs hasn't helped, she is now taking out her anxiety on the kitchen cabinets.

"You just told me things a mother doesn't want to hear, and now you expect me to just let you do things in the dark that you shouldn't even be allowed to do during the day?" Gwinnor again pulls open a cabinet and, with much clanking, takes out a teapot and two mugs. "Do you really think I'm going to wave you off smiling? I want to protect you and keep you here, that's what I want to do."

The kettle is her next victim. Angry, she snatches it from its stand and holds it murderously under the flowing jet of cold water.

"Grandma says I have no choice." Rowin looks pleadingly at Moree, hoping she can help her. "I'd rather not be doing it either, but both Granny and Aintín say I'm the only one who can fix this."

With a jerk, Gwinnor turns around. "Ma, tell me there's another solution than sending your only granddaughter into the woods to bury an evil spirit."

She looks wildly around the kitchen, as if expecting that by some miracle she might suddenly see her mother. "Can't I go with her or something like that, so I can protect her?"

Moree looks resignedly at the ground. "It's not my first choice either, child," she says softly to Rowin, as if Gwinnor could hear her. Her granddaughter's story of the creepy shadow grips her more than she wants to admit. Until now, she estimated Erris as a vengeful child who wanted to thwart his parents, but Aintín's words seem to warn of more than that. "But coming along is totally pointless. You can't see what she sees. So how will you help? You would only be getting in the way."

Rowin passively conveys the message to her mother, who reacts exactly as she expects.

"It's not happening! Do you hear? It. Is. Not. Happening." Facing Rowin, Gwinnor stands with her arms crossed, her face contorted in a mixture of fear and anger.

Helplessly, Rowin looks at Moree, but she gently shakes her head. "There's no point in standing up to her when she's in such a mood," she warns her granddaughter. "Then there's just no talking to her. Let her cool down. We'll see tomorrow."

Rowin looks at her in disbelief. She wants to scream. What will happen to the Count tonight? But she keeps quiet out of fear that Gwinnor will get even angrier.

"All right," Rowin admits. She lets her shoulders

hang down resignedly and drops her head with a nod. "I get it. You don't want me wandering around in the dark. That our graveyard is in danger, you just conveniently forget. But it's all right. I'll go to my room." With a wonderful sense of drama, she slowly stoops to the ground and strokes Zombie's head. "No, Zombie. We're not allowed to leave. Maybe tomorrow."

"I'm not buying this victimhood of yours, young lady." Gwinnor's voice sounds sharp. "It's my job as your mother to protect you, including from yourself. So that's what I'm doing right now."

Without looking back, Rowin walks out of the kitchen, down the hallway, and up the spiral staircase to her room. She is angry, disappointed, and relieved at the same time. Even if you weren't a scaredy-cat like her, the past events would have been enough to scare you to death. To be honest, she's not really looking forward to being bombarded as the savior of the world by going to bury Erris under a sacred oak tree.

Zombie walks happily into her room and lies down on his dog bed.

"Yeah, you just go ahead and be a good boy," Rowin grumbles. She takes off her shoes and drops down on her bed. "Then I'll be the scapegoat." She lays her head on her pillow and looks up at the ceiling. Her eyes burn as if some dirt has gotten in them and her eyelids become heavy. "I'll close my eyes for a minute, Zombie," she mutters.

She slowly opens the door of the mausoleum. It's quiet. Too quiet. She carefully pokes her head around the door and looks inside. There is no trace of the Count and Countess. All she hears is Erris' dismal laughter echoing hollowly against the bare walls. Large and small shards lie scattered across the floor. She feels lightheaded as soon as she steps inside. She doesn't want to enter, but she has to. It's as if her legs are made of lead, because she almost can't get one foot in front of the other. Her arms don't want what she wants either. She turns her head to the left and sees little Zombie lying dead-still in the corner. She wants to run to him, but she can't seem to move. She wants to scream, but she has no voice. Just as she wants to turn around to stumble outside, she is grabbed by her arms and lifted up. In front of her appears the hate-stricken face of Erris who, wide-eyed and foaming at the mouth, spins her around like a madman until she loses consciousness.

She must have dozed off, because she wakes up with her head pushed into her pillow and her cheeks wet with tears. Panting, she sits up. Zombie is squeaking anxiously with his paws against her bed. Not yet trusting her legs enough to stand up, she speaks to him reassuringly from her bedside. "I'm all right, Zombie. I'm fine." She doesn't actually believe it herself, and Zombie isn't really convinced either, as he remains where he is. "I had a bad dream," she continues. "I'm not quite sure what kind of dream, a nightmare or a prophecy, but it was terrifying to say the least."

Still a little shaky, Rowin gets up and walks to the window. Outside, the wind has died down and the moon is full and bright up in the sky. The graveyard looks peaceful and deserted. There is no evidence of her strange experiences earlier that evening. Yet it troubles her.

"I have to do something, Zombie." She sighs deeply and turns around. Leaning against the windowsill, she looks at her spectral friend. "I didn't get that dream without a reason. Erris isn't going to wait. I have no idea what he's up to, but if I'm to believe Aintín, it's not good. She talked about a shadow that wants to conquer the world. That has to be Erris. I have to do what she said, Zombie. I must bury his bones in that sacred place, or the Count will never be able to go to the Beyond. All this misery the Count is in now was caused by my stupid fault, so I'll have to make amends."

Rowin straightens her shoulders and steps away from the windowsill. She grabs her shoes, sits down on the edge of her bed, and puts them on. From her closet, she grabs a warm sweater.

"I suggest we go to the forest first to find a sacred oak tree consecrated by a druid. No idea how I'm going to do that, but that seems to make the most sense." She slides the sweater down over her head and straightens it. "We should bring a shovel to dig a hole. And a piece of string to reseal the tarp with the bones in it." She grabs a thick, dark coat hanging over her desk chair and puts it on.

Satisfied with her plan, she looks at Zombie. "So, what do you think? Do I look all right for a night out?" Zombie wags his tail.

"Great. Then we're ready to go. Miss Scay Pants and her trusty zombie dog can go out and save the world."

If she hadn't been so scared, she would certainly have laughed at her own joke.

Chapter 18

Fortunately, Rowin's mother is not awakened by the squeaky front door. She never pays any attention to it during the day, but now the sound is so loud, she's sure it can be heard even in the graveyard. With a pounding heart, Rowin waits for her angry mother in pajamas who will scold her and slam the door shut again, but nothing of the sort happens. Relieved, she sneaks out on tiptoes, gently closing the door behind her and hurrying down the high stairs.

Luckily, her bicycle is still outside on the driveway. For a piece of twine and a shovel, she has to go into the open shed that was once used by Rufus to store his machines. Now only the lawnmower is still there, a sort of small tractor that she sometimes gets to ride in the summer to mow the large lawn around the house. But to get to the barn, she'll have to walk across the gravel that lies beneath her mother's open bedroom window. Rowin takes three deep breaths in and out. Like a jaguar on the hunt who won't let a twig crack under their paws, she puts her feet on the gravel step by step. She makes sure to distribute her weight in such a way that the gravel collapses minimally and therefore makes almost no noise. Faster than expected, she arrives at the barn. Carefully, she walks around the small tractor to the back wall, where the loose tools hang.

The full moon illuminates about half of the barn. To see what she's doing, Rowin turns on the flashlight on her phone. She is startled by the bright light and quickly dims it by placing her hand over it. The last thing she wants is to draw attention to herself.

As quietly as possible, she removes the shovel from the wall. On the workbench next to it is a piece of string that she quickly rolls up and puts in her pocket. Then she turns off the flashlight and puts her phone back in her pocket. She notices that it is easier to walk from the dark part of the barn to the light than the other way around.

With the shovel in one hand and her bicycle in the other, she walks across the grass to the road, fearing that the stones on the driveway will give her away. Only the last two meters she has to cross the stones, but that is sufficiently far away from the bedrooms so no one will hear her.

The shovel poses some problems when she wants to hop on her bicycle, so she ties it to the carrier and under her seat with the twine. Satisfied with the result, she rides off into the dark night.

Zombie has been walking beside her the whole way. As if he knew they were on a dangerous mission, he didn't bark once. Grandma was right; he's perked up and all the way back to his old self. Rowin is glad to have him along. The howling wind sounds dreary in the silent forest, and in the dark every shadow looks like a scary monster.

"Keep your head cool and your brain focused," she says softly, more to herself than to Zombie.

"Don't forget that the real monster is in the mausoleum."

She looks around. To her great relief, she noticed yesterday that the deciduous trees are more on the edge of the forest, so she doesn't have to go to the middle, where the forest is at its darkest.

"We'll have to look hard, Zombie." Rowin brakes and gets off her bike. "Because I just haven't the faintest idea what to look for." She walks a bit off the path and parks her bike against one of the trees. "Or do you know by heart which of these trees is an oak?" She pulls her phone out of her pocket and types *oak tree* on Google. The pictures all show beautifully green and full trees with their distinctive leaves.

"That doesn't really help in the dark," Rowin grumbles. "Besides, it's spring and there are no leaves on them yet. Oh, wait, this is kind of interesting. We're looking for a big, thick tree, Zombie. And often underneath it seems to be barren ground because nothing can grow there because of its thick foliage." She gives him a hasty nod. "That's the way to quick learning."

As soon as she has put her phone away, she takes the shovel off her bike and walks into the woods. The full moon has kept everything well-lit so far, but now that she's under the trees it's getting darker and there's no path she can easily walk on. Instead, fallen branches and low bushes tug at her pants and socks. A single branch manages to penetrate her skin and causes a vicious scratch with a trickle of blood. She feels it but pays no attention. Zombie is not bothered by anything and continues to walk silently beside her.

Not only does the wind rustle the last leaves on the ground; every now and then Rowin hears an animal scurry away, though she doesn't see it. With each sound, her heart skips a beat and she pauses to gather courage. She walks deeper and deeper into the forest, until Zombie suddenly stops and begins to growl softly.

"What is it?" whispers Rowin. Startled, she looks in the direction to which Zombie is growling, his white hair standing straight up. At first she sees nothing, but then she notices the faint glow that she thought was moonshine. She tries to get a better look at the soft light by staring at it intently. It doesn't work: it remains vague.

Open up and use your power. It is the voice of Aintín.

Surprised, Rowin looks around. "Aintín?" she whispers softly. "Are you here? What should I do?"

Open up and use your power, Aintín's voice says again.

"How?" Out of fear and frustration, she almost begins to scream. Just in time, she is able to slap a hand in front of her mouth. Wide-eyed, she sees the already faint glow become even paler.

Believe in your strength! Aintín's voice also ebbs away.

"No, no, no!" squeaks Rowin. "Don't go away! Help me, Aintín! What power? What do I have to do?"

Almost inaudibly, the last words dance on the waves of the rushing wind towards her.

Believe in yourself!

Rowin bites her lower lip softly with her front teeth and tries to swallow. Her dry mouth refuses, making it seem more like she is choking. The glow has almost completely disappeared now. She has no idea what to do, and in a panic she squeezes her eyes tightly shut. Instantly, everything around her changes. The wind sounds very distant, as if filtered through a hundred layers of cotton wool.

Zombie's growling has become a soft tinkling sound, like the wind chime in the garden that chimes with the lightest summer breeze. From behind her eyelids, she sees a vivid light, changing from bright white to rainbow colors. Very carefully, she relaxes her eye muscles and she slowly peeks through her eyelashes.

The darkness is not as dark as it was a moment ago. It seems like a soft, light blue line is moving through the forest. Instinctively, Rowin knows she must follow this line. She opens her eyes and wants to tell Zombie to stay with her, but everything seems to be happening in slow motion. The line is moving farther and farther away from her, and Rowin understands that she can't waste time.

Hoping that Zombie will follow at his own pace, she shifts off to run after the soft blue light.

With the first step, she already feels that her feet aren't really touching the ground anymore. It feels more like floating than running. Only the tips of her shoes still make contact with the ground, and her steps are three times bigger than normal. Her fear is gone, and she enjoys the strange feeling of moving this way. If she had to race against the world sprinting champion now, she would win with ease.

After a dozen or so of these "flying steps," the trees are wider apart and she comes to a clearing. The line lingers for a moment and then dissolves. The hum in her head, which she thought was the wind, is louder here. Now that she's listening more closely, she can hear it's a rarefied, monotonous chant.

Before her in the forest looms a kind of procession of vague, pale figures in long robes. She is not afraid, but just to be sure, she hides behind a tree. Zombie has followed her and comes to sit beside her, panting.

She looks at him for a moment and then slowly puts a finger to her lips. *Do. Not. Bark. Now.*

Chapter 19

The front three figures are bearded and wear a robe down to the ground, tied around their waists with a string belt. One holds a torch; the other two hold a pointed stick in one hand and a sickle-shaped knife in the other. Behind them walk five women. Their clothes also fall to the ground, but these dresses are not as shapeless as the men's: they are decorated with stones and feathers.

Around the neck of one of the women hangs an amber stone, which suspiciously resembles the stone on Gwinnor's necklace. From the way they walk and proudly look straight ahead, Rowin understands that they are the really important figures in this little gathering, and that the men are only there as indispensable defenders in this dark forest. These are druids! These are her ancestors, the people she is descended from! The people who were also called priests or healers and who had an important role in their society.

The druids walk purposefully to one of the largest trees in the clearing and kneel down reverently at its base. The women's chanting turns into the rhythmic recitation of text in a language similar to what she heard earlier that day at Aintín's grave. Only this time she sees the words floating through the forest, as if someone were simultaneously typing a subtitle with their laptop. And strangely enough, she also understands what is being said.

The woman nearest to the tree stands up and raises her hands to the sky.

"Cran darach naofa," the woman says imploringly. "Tugann do thalamh coisricthe neart..."

Rowin is only half listening, reading along in the air. "O sacred oak, your hallowed ground gives us strength and wisdom to govern our people. May your holiness forever fill your humble servants with your..."

Zombie's excited yapping puts an end to the performance. He had listened nicely when Rowin asked, but now the tension was getting too much for him. He could have just about handled the sight of the kneeling people, but that shouting woman with her arms in the air looks like a threat. Barking, he runs toward the druids.

"No! Zombie, no!" screams Rowin, but it's already too late. The text and the people vanish into thin air, as does the pale blue glow with which the forest was lit. Zombie is now freakishly barking at nobody.

Her head feels light. Her arms and legs regain their normal weight and she hears the wind instead of the female druid's voice. For a brief moment, she wonders how it is possible that she understands and comprehends all this, until she realizes that time is running out and she must act.

"Bad boy," she grumbles to Zombie as she stands beside him in the clearing. She looks at the broad trunk of the imposing tree in front of her. "Sorry, your Holiness," she begins clumsily. "I must dig a grave at your feet for an evil spirit. Otherwise, his spirit will never find rest and then I can never save my graveyard..." She pauses for a moment. If she is using this sacred ground only for the good of her graveyard, it would sound very selfish. "...and the whole world," she concludes her argument. She has no idea if it's really true, but it sounds very plausible at the moment.

She doesn't know why, but she is waiting for an approving sign from the tree. Expectantly, she cranes her neck to look at the crown swaying back and forth high in the air. Is it her imagination, or does it bend a little towards her, making it look like it's nodding yes? Rowin thinks the sign is clear enough and puts her shovel in the ground to dig a hole big and deep enough for a bag of bones to disappear for eternity.

Digging a hole in the ground is hard work, but digging a hole in wet ground is almost impossibly hard, Rowin finds out. She had to take off her coat and sweater after only ten minutes of shoveling, that's how hot she got. At home, the heaviest thing she lifts is a thick book from the top shelf in the library room, so her body hasn't really been able to train for this task. She wipes the sweat from her forehead and, like an experienced gardener, puts her weight onto the handle of her shovel, which she has set halfway into the ground. She takes a panting breath as she looks contentedly at the result of her hard work.

"Not bad for an amateur, if I may say so myself."

Rowin places her shovel on the edge of the hole and steps out. The wind makes her soggy T-shirt, which has been pulled out of her pants because of the hard work, flutter. She shivers as she feels the cold night air on her wet body. Quickly she puts her sweater and coat back on.

"If you thought this was already hard work, Zombie," she says to her doggie ponderingly, "then you shouldn't think about what is yet to come." With a deep sigh, she turns around. "Find your way back to my bicycle, boy. Search!"

Without hesitation, Zombie walks back to the bike in a straight line, and Rowin follows her four-legged friend. Pedaling is a lot easier now that she doesn't have to keep checking if the shovel is still there. She can see she's almost at the cemetery again. The knot in her stomach has grown larger during the ride and she feels a vague nausea coming on. Yet she bravely pedals on down the narrow side road. She parks her bike against a tree about where she stopped yesterday. Because she is not in as much of a hurry as last time, she is able to crawl under the barbed wire without getting hurt. Zombie runs ahead of her across the meadow. The light of the full moon shines ghostly across the grass, and the top of the hedge stands out black against the softly lit background. Once they reach the fence, they are in for an unpleasant surprise.

"Geez, how stupid!" Rowin slaps her forehead with her hand. "Of course, I could have imagined that a cemetery would be closed at night." She takes a few steps back and looks at the stone columns from which the fences hang. The columns, like the fences, are too high to climb over. She walks back and tries to squeeze her body between the bars. They are too close together to let an adult through, but she is a slim teenager. She manages to get her shoulder and hip to the other side, but her head is different story. Frustrated, she pulls back half her body.

"If I can't get through, Zombie, I most certainly can't manage to push that bag of bones through."

Rowin clenches her fists and squeezes so hard that her nails press deep welts into her palm.

Annoyed, she blows through her clenched jaw. Angrily, she kicks at an unsuspecting pebble that has the audacity to lay at her feet. She has come so far and now she is stopped by a stupid fence!

"This is not going to happen," she hisses. Determined not to let anything stop her, she steps toward the gate. As she grasps the latch, she sees a white figure appear from behind the gate, approaching with haste. He is wearing a cap and a porter's uniform, and from his belt hangs a large bunch of keys. He rattles the bunch and grabs out a large key, which he inserts into the lock. A soft click sounds and the gate swings open.

"How…" Overwhelmed, Rowin steps into the cemetery. Only now does she see the other residents standing there who, almost invisible because of the white moonlight, seem to be waiting for her. Spectral children take shelter under their mothers' skirts and phantasmal women lean on their pale husbands, weeping.

"Help us," the gatekeeper begs. "Please."

Chapter 20

Rowin opens her mouth to say something, but a howl that gives her goosebumps silences the words before they can come out. The residents of the cemetery rush in all directions, seeking shelter in their safe burial chambers. A little higher up the hill, two white wolves scurry among the graves, clearly visible.

Occasionally, they push their paws into the grass and sniff at a tombstone. Then suddenly they raise their heads as if they hear something from an invisible sign and run to the top of the hill.

Rowin stands as though she were nailed to the ground. What is this? This doesn't square at all with the vision she had at her graveyard. These wolves are white instead of black! They don't have red eyes and they don't destroy anything. Besides, they are roaming here and not at her graveyard. Rowin tries to sort out her thoughts by shaking her head. So, what else was wrong with her prediction? Uncertainly, she looks at the hill again, but there is no trace of the wolves.

Rowin slides the sleeve of her coat up a bit, grabs a piece of bare skin near her wound from the construction fence, puts her nails in it, and squeezes as hard as she can. She suppresses a scream as a vicious pain cuts through her arm. No, she's not dreaming then. Zombie squeaks behind her, and when she turns around, she sees him standing behind her with his tail between his legs.

"I don't have to ask if you saw them too," she mutters. "You'd almost forget why we're here."

The gatekeeper hesitantly comes walking out of the bushes. "Do something," he says hastily but forcefully. "You have put us in this danger. Now get us out again." Rowin wants to protest, but the gatekeeper raises his hand to silence her. "You brought him here, with his vicious, negative energy and his out-of-control fleabags with their sharp teeth. You dragged us into something we want nothing to do with. We have no idea why you did that, we just know we're in a lot of trouble now."

The gatekeeper doesn't sound angry but rather tired and sad. Rowin droops her shoulders and lowers her eyes. Just now in the woods, she had been able to take on the whole world. She had been strong and decisive. Now there is nothing left of that. This is all her fault! By bringing the bones of Erris here, she has brought misery to this cemetery. She thought the vision had been clear: make sure the Count finds what he is looking for so he can go to the Beyond. Only then will you protect your graveyard from the destruction of the scary beasts.

But it's not that easy at all. She has found what the Count was looking for, only he and Erris don't even want to be near each other! She's made a mess of things, when all she wanted to do was help. She *had* to help even, as her grandmother told her. As if it was easy to be told at thirteen that fate has bombed you into being a lifesaver. As if she would want that!

She feels something strange bubbling up in her chest. Guilt, anger, and fear merge into an overpowering feeling that she cannot describe, because she has never felt it before. She just stands there, frozen in time and space.

The woman in front of her has the same face as Aintín, but she is much younger. Her hair dances in long, golden tufts around her head, which looks absolutely nothing like the snake head with bat nests anymore. Her skin shines in the sun and her cheeks are pinkish red as she smiles at Rowin. Her dress fans around her body as she spins and dances and claps her hands above her head. She holds out her hands in an attempt to entice Rowin to dance with her. When Rowin doesn't move with her, the young Aintín takes a few steps forward. She strikes the four dots under Rowin's eyes with her index fingers and gives her a gentle squeeze on both cheeks.

"Don't be so gloomy, dear. Everyone dances their own dance in life. Dance your dance with confidence and you'll be a dancer. If you don't move, you'll never learn."

Rowin doesn't move. The beautiful woman now looks at her urgently. "Go," she says. Slowly, her face grows whiter and older, until she looks like the old Aintín. "You can do this."

The gatekeeper clears his throat and tilts his head slightly. "You okay?" he asks Rowin. She slowly nods yes. The flash of young Aintín still echoes in her mind. She's right: she mustn't give up now. She must dance her dance, as the young woman so beautifully put it.

The bubbling sensation in her chest grows stronger and spreads to the rest of her body. Rowin straightens her shoulders and raises her chin in the air. She doesn't know where it comes from, but a strange calm descends on her.

"Okay, Zombie," she says combatively. "We'll give that skeleton a run for its money." Before the gatekeeper can say anything else, she walks along the first graves and up the hill with Zombie right behind her.

Before she has to cross the clearing to the Count's mausoleum, she stops, having crept from gravestone to gravestone, wary of wolves. Now she stands on a plaque behind an immensely large headstone, panting from the steep climb. She nods to the resident, who pokes his head out to see who has the audacity to stand on his grave, and puts a finger to her lips. The head quickly shoots back down. Rowin looks cautiously from behind the stone to the mausoleum. It is well guarded by about four white wolves who, slightly bored, are strolling back and forth in front of the entrance. Occasionally, they snap at each other just to have something to do. The door is still half open, exactly as she left it yesterday after her flight. A bright light streams out, occasionally interspersed with a flash. It seems that the Count and his son are still measuring their strength against each other.

"I have good news and I have bad news, Zombie," she whispers to her dog who is faithfully waiting at her feet.

"The good news is that Erris apparently hasn't defeated his father yet." She waits a moment before continuing. "The bad news is that there are four spirit wolves keeping watch and I have no idea how to get into the mausoleum to get those bones."

Rowin looks around. She has a hunch and looks for something to throw. Next to the plaque are some pebbles. She bends down and picks one up. "This always works in movies. It's all about distraction, Zombie. Pay attention." She looks to see where the wolves are and aims the pebble across the clearing against a tombstone. A loud *pok* sounds and the alarmed wolves look to the side where the sound is coming from. One of them runs at a trot to the tombstone to investigate what is going on, but the other three remain standing in front of the mausoleum.

"Alright then, so that doesn't work." Disappointed at the result, Rowin leans her back against the stone. "Wait." She bends down again and grabs as many pebbles from the ground as she can hold in one hand. Again, she throws the pebbles to the other side, where now six *pok* sounds reverberate against different stones. This time three wolves go to investigate.

"Bah, I was convinced it would work," she whispers softly. She continues to watch the wolves, who are already walking back. "We'll have to come up with something much better, Zombie. But what?"

Zombie looks at her, wagging his tail as he gives a lick over her hand. He doesn't hesitate for a moment. Before she can stop him, his little white shadow shoots down her leg. Horrified, Rowin watches her best friend run into the clearing, stared at hungrily by eight bloodthirsty eyes.

Chapter 21

"Zombie! No!" whispers Rowin hoarsely as she bites down hard on her fist to prevent herself from screaming. The wolves see the little dog running across the grass to the other side and stand stock-still with pricked ears. Zombie tries to lure the monsters as far away from Rowin as possible, so he lingers for a moment in the middle of the clearing, barking defiantly at the motionless creatures.

That's too much for the white wolves' hunting instincts, and with a loud howl they set off in pursuit.

Through a haze of tears, Rowin watches her little friend disappear among the dark gravestones with four experienced hunters right behind him. She has no time to dwell on the danger Zombie is in. She knows she must take advantage of this opportunity, or Zombie will have exposed himself to this peril for nothing. She stumbles from behind the headstone and runs as fast as she can to the open door of the mausoleum.

The noise coming from the burial chamber reveals that the Count and his son are not using their powers to settle their argument with words. She carefully pokes her head a little way around the door and sees that Erris is standing with his back towards her. He is bombarding his father with earth and stones with an evil pleasure. So, not much has changed since she fled.

She notices that the Count, quite visible, is still protesting weakly, although he is in no condition to resist for long.

"Come on, Papa. Where's your famous fighting spirit?" taunts Erris. "You used to be able to talk down the tenants if they dared to contradict you. You were always so proud of your unscrupulous way of ruling over your peasants, who you squeezed to desperation. He who will not hear must feel, right? I was so looking forward to a good fight, but you're only a shadow of the hard brute I remember." Erris loosens his grip a little so that less sand and stones reach the exhausted Count.

Rowin looks for the Countess, but she is nowhere to be seen. She suspects that she has fled to the safety of her tomb because of the fierce battle between her son and husband. In the distance, Rowin hears the wolves howling and she feels a shudder run through her body. She must hurry.

The bones are exactly where she left them. Erris doesn't pay special attention, but she's sure he'll notice if she starts reaching for them. When she looks at the fighting men again, her gaze crosses that of the Count. For a moment his eyes light up, as if he knows why she has come back. Without alerting Erris of her presence, he immediately looks back at his son with cold-hearted eyes, straightening up to try and hold Erris' attention.

"A nobleman must always rule with a tough hand," the Count says in a firm voice. "You will never understand that, Son. You think you are the same as me, but I have never slaughtered defenseless animals or helpless women like you did. I am a ruler. You are a monster. You had slipped into a dark place, under the influence of a dark force. I had no choice but to throw you in the dungeon. You violated every law that exists on this Earth. No one could save you when you sold your soul to Charon."

During the Count's long speech, Rowin moved closer inch by inch. She can almost touch the tarp and can see how hard the Count is trying to hold the attention of his son, who is growing restless at his words. Erris begins to pace back and forth a bit, and Rowin can feel his anger taking over.

"No child deserves to be thrown in the dungeon by his father," Erris shrieks when he notices that his father has not finished speaking yet. "You've said far too much already. You act like I was the only one who liked killing. I don't want to listen to your stupid stories anymore. I meant more to Charon than I ever meant to you!"

The moment Erris unleashes his anger on the last vestige of his father's resistance, Rowin seizes the opportunity and grabs the tarp with the bones on it. With blinding hatred, Erris tries to bury his father underneath earth and stones, while Rowin takes off with her precious cargo. As soon as she's out the door, she runs across the clearing to the shelter of the gravestones, meanwhile scanning for any sign of life from Zombie. All she hears is a four-part, triumphant, drawn-out howl. In misery, she squeezes her eyes tightly shut and immediately a bluish line shows her the quickest escape route. With the now familiar giant steps, she races downhill without once tripping over a pebble or a neglected grave. But at the entrance she suddenly stops as if struck by lightning.

The wolves stand close to the fence in a semicircle. They growl and snarl at each other, especially at one wolf, who is holding something in his mouth. Rowin's heart freezes. She knows exactly what the limp bundle is dangling halfway out of its mouth. Before she can do anything to save her little friend, she hears an icy scream. The wolves stop growling, put their ears to their necks, and run up the hill. Overhead an inky black sky rises, obscuring the moon and shrouding the cemetery in an ominous black darkness.

Erris has discovered that his bones are gone, Rowin realizes. She looks back at the hill and is torn by a terrible dilemma: should she go after the wolves and save Zombie, or should she bury the bones and save her graveyard? The faces of her grandmother and Cara come to her mind and she knows she has no choice. She squeezes her eyes shut again and follows the blue line to her bike with giant strides. Big tears roll down her cheeks and some of them get stuck in her sweater. She has never felt this lonely.

Her bicycle is patiently waiting for her. Rowin puts the tarp on the ground so she can tie it up before attaching it to her bike rack. She frantically searches for the piece of twine she had put in her pocket in the shed that night.

"Oh no," she groans. She had used the twine to tie the shovel. It was probably still on the ground somewhere by the oak tree.

The howls of the wolves sound frighteningly close.

"No time left," she mutters. "I'll pick up my bike later." Trusting her new gift, she squeezes her eyes shut and follows the blue line to show her the quickest way to the sacred site, which apparently runs straight through the forest. As with the shadow at her graveyard, she does not only feel the presence of the wolves, but she can see them from above, running between the trees. Erris follows like a rabid bull, throwing anything towards her he can get his hands on.

Rowin's strides are large and she is quite fast, but the wolves and Erris are getting closer and closer. Erris in particular becomes more powerful the closer he gets to his bones. She hears him cursing and ranting, which reminds her of his foaming face in her dream. Occasionally, something ricochets against the tarp bag. She has no time to think about it and speeds between the branches, blindly trusting the soft blue light. Erris must be close, because she feels herself being slowed down, as if someone had hung something heavy on the bag. And the wolves are only about ten meters away from her. Rowin is panting heavily. All she can hear is the loud thumping of her heart in her ears. Her legs feel like lead and she can definitely feel that she has been on the move for almost twenty-four hours. She fights her way through the brushwood, which the wolves easily cross. She should be there any second now! Any second!

Rowin can see how Erris has caught up with the wolves and is extending his fingers to grab the tarp and pull her to the ground. In a last-ditch effort to stop her, he topples a young tree in front of her. She can just barely avoid it, but she wastes precious seconds. The unexpected movement almost makes her lose her balance and she comes dangerously close to the clacking jaws of one of the wolves. At last she sees the end of the blue line. That must be the sacred oak. Just two more paces, one more…

"Never in a million years!" shouts Erris, when he sees where they are. He gets a hold of a tip of the tarp and pulls as hard as he can.

Chapter 22

The jerk brings Rowin to a stop in one fell swoop. Her left leg is just inside the circular clearing around the oak tree. The rest of her body is still outside the circle. Instinctively, she turns around on her one leg with a nifty move, bringing most of her back into the circle. She holds the bag, which first dangled on her back, firmly with two hands in front of her belly, a few inches away from the circle. Rowin puts her heels in the sand, pulling as hard as she can at the bag of bones.

Erris pulls just as hard the opposite way. To her surprise, she notices how the wolves stop in front of the clearing. Erris, too, remains in place outside the circle.

"Let go!" Erris brings his furious face to within a few millimeters of Rowin's. "Let go before I crush you." Rowin looks anxiously at the frenzied look in his eyes and his grimacing mouth. She has just heard about his ancient atrocities in the mausoleum, so she takes his threat very seriously. But letting go is not an option. Not now that she has come this far. Not now that the pit she dug is only a few feet away, waiting for the rattling bones of this evil spirit. She's so close.

Rowin strains all her muscles and pulls with all her might. Yet she feels Erris gaining ground millimeter by millimeter. He is too strong. The wolves run restlessly back and forth, howling along the edge of the clearing. Again she is surprised that they do not step into the circle to attack her.

The largest of the four wolves is also the bravest. He hesitates for a second before stepping into the circle to devour her with his imposing jaws. As soon as his front paw comes into contact with the bare ground around the sacred oak tree, it begins to hiss and smoke. A painful howl echoes through the forest and the wolf immediately withdraws his paw.

Rowin opens her eyes wide. The flash has surprised her, but it also clarifies a lot. Now she understands why no one is attacking her. Not only the oak tree, but also the ground around it is sacred. That's why Erris and the wolves won't enter the circle!

Rejuvenated by this realization, Rowin fixes her tormentor with a steely glare. She is no longer afraid. Erris sees her triumphant gaze and is disturbed by it. For only half a second his grip on the tarp slackens. It is enough for Rowin who, determined to win the battle, throws her body backwards in an unexpected movement with all the strength she has left. She rolls backward into the circle when Erris releases the bag. Screeching and cursing her, he floats back and forth in front of the clearing, followed by his squealing and howling wolves. Panting, Rowin sits on the ground, watching the scene. Astonished that she won the pulling contest, she can't believe she got off unscathed. She looks at the tarp that has fallen half open, leaving a few bones scattered around her. She realizes she shouldn't stupidly stay put. The longer she waits, the more time Erris has to contrive a ruse.

Quickly she gets up, picks up the bones, and throws them into the tarp with the rest. She watches as Erris holds up his hands, making the young, fallen tree from earlier float above the ground.

Rowin doesn't think twice and runs with the bones to the pit she has dug. She can hear the tree trunk whizzing towards her and, at the last moment, she dives forward into the open hole. The tree whooshes over her, bounces against the oak tree, and falls right across the opening of the pit.

Rowin looks up and is relieved to see that the young tree is not covering the entire hole. She stands up, grabs the bottom of the tarp, and lifts it up so all the bones fall out. As soon as the last bone hits the bottom of the pit, the earth begins to shake. Rowin almost loses her balance. She seeks support against the wall of the deep pit, which slowly begins to collapse.

"If you enjoy digging a grave so much, you can rest in it yourself," Erris shouts hysterically from the forest. With all his strength, he shoves the excavated soil, which lies next to the pit, over Rowin.

Fighting against the dark earth, she grabs hold of the tree trunk. The heavy weight of the shifting soil pulls her body down with it, and she can feel her legs getting more and more stuck in the deep pit.

Coughing because of the small pieces of earth that penetrate her lungs, she pulls herself up as far as she can. Dead tired, she manages to pull her upper body over the tree, while her legs get buried deeper and deeper in the half-collapsed pit. She has given everything she's got, but her strength is slowly draining away. Exhausted, she tries to lift her head, but it falls down limply. Everything she has done has been for nothing.

"Sorry, Grandma," she mutters defeatedly, before slowly losing consciousness.

Erris triumphantly shouts out a victory cry. Because of the sacred circle, he can't get to Rowin, but the fact that she is hanging lifeless over the tree trunk gives him a fantastic feeling. He looks at his wolves and lets out a devilish laugh.

"So you thought you could outsmart me." Erris gasps with excitement and his eyes sparkle feverishly. "I am invincible! I won't let a measly little kid like you stop me!" He drums his hands against his chest, his face contorted into a frenzied grimace.

"And to prove that you are nothing at all, I will crush your body against your sacred oak tree."

Erris stands in front of the circle with his hands raised and throws his head back. "Look at your master, look what I do to people who get in my way," he shouts in a sinister voice. He turns his head to Rowin and makes a lifting gesture with his arms, as if to lift the tree trunk Rowin is hanging on.

Nothing happens.

Once again, he roughly raises his arms and tries to get the log up. His arms tremble with the effort, but the trunk does not move. Furious, he lets out a bloodcurdling cry and makes uncontrolled movements with his arms. The wolves watch the scene with their ears flattened against their heads and shuffle restlessly back and forth. Realizing that his powers are gone, Erris looks frantically at the collapsed pit where Rowin's body is still hanging lifelessly. In his blind revenge, he has buried not only Rowin but also his own bones.

Erris' long, furious cry slowly dies away as his spectral appearance dissolves among the trees. The wolves walk dazedly across the spot where their leader just stood and squeal softly. They take one last look at Rowin's motionless body before disappearing into the forest, whimpering in their wake.

Chapter 23

When Rowin regains consciousness, the forest is silent. A streak of silver moonlight shines on her arm. She looks at it in wonder. As soon as it dawns on her that the inky black sky has disappeared, she lifts her head and looks around. The trees murmur softly. She scans the surroundings for any sign of Erris or his wolves, afraid that they might be hiding somewhere, but the forest remains empty. The moon shines kindly on the clearing, but some bright spots in the sky are a reminder that a new day is about to begin.

Rowin tries to get up by pressing her arms against the tree trunk. A twinge of pain travels through her abdomen and chest. She must have been hanging on this tree trunk for much longer than she thought. She pulls a rueful face when she tries to push herself up, held back by her legs that are buried under the soil. She attempts to pull up one leg, which miraculously succeeds with some wriggling back and forth. She notices that falling pebbles and soil immediately fill the hole where her leg had just been, and she feels her other leg loosen as a result. With some effort, she pulls that one out of the ground as well. She places her left knee on the tree trunk and her right foot next to her hand. Then she carefully rises to her feet and leaps like a tiger to the safer ground of the clearing.

She turns to the spot where she had just been lying with her legs buried in the ground and looks at the loosened earth. Slowly it dawns on her that Erris is underneath that layer of soil. Her mission is accomplished! She cannot suppress a smile. She may have dug the pit, but in his attempt to destroy her, he just eliminated himself.

Rowin inhales the smell of the damp forest ground, which at this moment smells more delicious than the most expensive perfume in the world. Her clothes are covered in sand and mud, as are her face and hands. She doesn't even want to think about what her long hair looks like and how long it will take her to get all the tangles out. She suspects that she probably looks more like Aintín now than she ever thought she would.

Automatically, she searches the environment for a small white shadow that usually is close to her. As soon as the terrible image of the wolf with Zombie's limp body in its mouth comes back to mind, she feels a sharp pain in her chest. Her dear, loyal friend sacrificed himself for the greater cause. She feels warm tears draw narrow stripes down her earth-covered cheeks. Dear, sweet Zombie. Without his brave act, she would never have been able to bury Erris.

Feeling empty inside, Rowin walks to the oak tree and picks up the shovel that lies on the ground. She turns to the pit that is already mostly filled in. She decides to take no chances and begins to fill the pit to the brim with fresh earth. Erris' bones must never, ever surface again. Finally, Rowin looks at the spot with satisfaction that no one will suspect that the skeleton of an evil spirit was buried there last night. She tries to recreate the natural environment as much as possible by sprinkling leaves and branches over the freshly dug earth, making it look exactly like the ground at the base of every tree in the forest. The first light of day peeks between the tops of the trees. The growling of her stomach does not surprise her. Her legs have been trembling for some time now, indicating that her body has exerted itself immensely and is longing for something in return. She has to go home and eat something or she will literally faint from hunger.

She looks back at the hidden spot on the ground one more time. It is okay now. Erris is defeated, the wolves are gone, and the inky black sky has receded. She has done everything she needed to do to save her family's graveyard.

She brushes off the last earthly residue from her clothes and wipes her hands on her jeans. The first steps she takes are a little uncertain, but soon she is walking firmly back to the cemetery, back to her bike. Her mother and her grandmother will have no idea what's been keeping her so long.

***

Rowin has never seen her mother as happy as she is now. She has barely walked into the hall before Gwinnor is standing in front of her with tearful eyes.

"Oh, my little girl!" Gwinnor cries in relief. "Where were you? Your bed was empty when I tried to wake you up early this morning. What have you been doing? Where have you been? Why didn't you tell me? I was so worried!"

Rowin doesn't answer any of her mother's questions. And Gwinnor doesn't seem to expect it either, for she continues to talk to her uninterruptedly as she takes her daughter to the kitchen.

Moree is standing against the kitchen counter, waiting for Rowin with her arms crossed and a tense face. She would love to put her hands against Rowin's head to read her mind and see everything that has happened last night, but Gwinnor claims her daughter all to herself. It's logical but rather inconvenient at this moment.

"Any luck?" is the only thing Moree asks Rowin, right through Gwinnor's rattling. Rowin just nods before being pushed into a chair by her mother, who hugs her and kisses her on the forehead.

"Promise me you'll never do anything like that again," Gwinnor says in a punitive tone, rubbing a tear from the corner of her eye. "I went almost crazy with fear."

Rowin nods again and looks at her mother and grandmother. "I buried Erris' bones in the forest," she says tonelessly. "Under a sacred oak, as Aintín said. Our graveyard is saved and Zombie has sacrificed himself for it."

Gwinnor slaps her hand in front of her mouth in

dismay, as does Moree, who hadn't missed the little dog until now.

"Oh, my dear," Gwinnor says with compassion as she strokes Rowin's hair. "That really saddens me."

"What happened?" asks Moree. Rowin looks wearily at both women, who are waiting tensely for more explanation. "I don't want to talk about it now. I want to eat, take a hot shower, and then I want to sleep. When I wake up, I'll tell you everything, okay?"

Gwinnor turns and grabs a bag of sandwiches lying on the counter. "I can't say I like having to wait such a long time for an explanation, but it's okay," she decides. "You can tell us all about it when you wake up."

Chapter 24

The next afternoon is a lovely spring day, and because it's already noon, the sunshine feels almost warm. Rowin is riding her bicycle again, on her way to the cemetery in Lordensland after sleeping for almost twenty-four hours.

This morning, she kept her promise by telling her distressed mother and her impatient grandmother all about her adventure, leaving no details behind. Then Moree took her to the graveyard, where Cara wrapped her ghostly arms around her neck and jumped in joy before Rowin told her story one more time to anyone who wanted to hear it. That turned out to be the whole graveyard. Cara had almost blushed with excitement when Rowin told them about the wolves and her battle with Erris at the pit, and everyone shed a tear when hearing about the heroic deed of "their" brave Zombie. Every so often Madam Curiosa shouted "Oh-la-la, ma chérie!" while holding her fan in front of her mouth in disgust, but her eyes were glazed with sensation. Moree had stood there proudly, nodding occasionally in agreement as if she had been there herself, but then again, she was hearing the story for the second time.

And now Rowin is on her way to see the Count. It's a strange feeling to be on the road without her canine companion. The first thing she did this morning was look at Zombie's empty dog bed, and even now she still has the impulse to call out his name. It's an emptiness she'll never be able to get used to.

The forest and the meadow look peaceful. Only a few raven-black hairs hang from the barbed wire, a reminder of what happened here yesterday. Rowin touches the sensitive spot on her head where the hairs pulled out. With mixed feelings, she follows the hedge to the gate, which is open again as if nothing had happened. The cemetery is crowded. Pale children are playing catch, yelling and trying to tap each other. Groups of phantasmal, well-dressed people are standing everywhere talking. The gatekeeper smiles contentedly at her as she walks by and taps his white cap in a friendly salute. The Count walks in the middle of the path while the Countess holds his arm. He is stopped by many people for a chat, which his wife seems to prefer to do more than him.

Rowin smiles contentedly. When she turns around to go home, the Count catches sight of her. He apologizes to the couple he is talking to and walks up to her. "Young lady," he speaks solemnly. "I want to thank you for what you have done for us." He gives a brief nod to his wife. "It was hard on her. I won't say I'm happy that our son can't lie with us, but to be honest I must say we had lost him a long time ago to dark forces stronger than us. We finally have peace now, and we owe it to you."

Like a farmer judging his cattle, his eyes glide over her face and linger on the four dots below her eyes.

Uncomfortably, Rowin shifts her weight onto her other foot. Perhaps Erris took more after his father than the Count was willing to admit.

"I can't say I enjoyed doing it," Rowin answers honestly. "For a moment, I thought I wouldn't live to tell the tale, and I also lost my best friend along the way." She swallows wearily and looks past the Count to the Countess, who suddenly looks old and tired. "But it had to be done and we both profited from it."

The Count gives her a puzzled look.

"It's a long story," Rowin concludes. "Something concerning my graveyard."

Count Gratema smiles and takes her hand, which immediately feels like it's pierced by a thousand tiny needles. "If we both have gained something from it, then that's even better," he assures her. "But don't just stand here at the gate. Come in! I'm not the only one who wants to shake your hand."

Rowin isn't exactly looking forward to an afternoon of piercing needles in her hands. Yet she follows him politely into the cemetery, where grateful residents immediately surround her.

She smiles kindly at everyone and shyly takes in all the compliments. The well-meant slaps on her shoulder feel like a pincushion's worth of needles being pushed into her skin, but she keeps grinning through it all.

After a few minutes, Rowin gets a strange feeling. She is sure that it's not caused by all the spectral contact. It's a weird feeling in her back, like someone is watching her.

Uncertainly, she turns her head and looks over her shoulder through the gate. The forest that lies at the bottom of the hill is as dark as ever; only the tops of the trees sway calmly in a gentle gust of wind. Other than that, nothing moves.

A shiver runs down her spine. *Don't act like that,* she addresses herself harshly. *The evil has been eliminated. You have won. Believe in yourself!*

A gentle prod on her arm brings her back to what she was doing: shaking the hands of ghosts. She turns her head back to the waiting, pale people and smiles. Today she gained many friends.

Epilogue

A dark figure stands hidden among the trees at the edge of the forest. His face is almost covered by a pointed hood attached to a wide-brimmed, black cloak. He holds a limp, white bundle tightly in his left hand. His eyes are fixed on Rowin's back, which moves gently back and forth with the shaking of all the phantasmal hands. Five large, black wolves roam around him, slyly looking around with their red eyes. The largest wolf, which almost reaches his waist, sits down next to him and follows his master's gaze.

"Look closely, Styx," the man says when he sees Rowin looking his way. He wraps his cloak a little tighter around him. "Look closely at her face."

With his right hand, he pulls the hood off his head in one fluid motion. His long, raven-black hair drops loosely around his face, which is hard and ruthless. His eyes are cold and almost black, but what stands out most are the dots beneath them. Under each eye there are four black dots that, if they had not been so symmetrically placed under each eye, could easily be mistaken for freckles.

Acknowledgements

I would like to thank my husband Peter for being my sparring partner and for giving me constructive feedback.

My publisher Sandra for believing in me and my manuscript.

My international marketing officer Melissa, for selling the rights to my book so it can be published in the USA.

My friends Jim and Ramsey, who helped me make this story a bit more American.

And AM Ink Publishing for believing in this book and making me an internationally published author.

Thank you all so very much!

About the Author

Marjo de Vroed is a Dutch author. *The Dark Vision* is the first book in a trilogy that she began writing after her career as an elementary teacher. Since then she has written multiple children's books.

If you want to know more you can visit her website or her social media pages: Instagram, Facebook or TikTok.

www.marjodevroed.com

www.ingramcontent.com/pod-product-compliance
Lightning Source LLC
LaVergne TN
LVHW090957080826
845145LV00003B/1036

* 9 7 8 1 9 5 8 8 4 2 6 3 8 *